I0760475

Southern Flames

A MAX PORTER PARANORMAL MYSTERY

Stuart Jaffe

Southern Flames is a work of fiction. Names, characters, places, and incidents either are the product of the author's imagination or are used fictitiously, and any resemblance to any persons, living or dead, business establishments, events, or locales is entirely coincidental.

SOUTHERN FLAMES

Cover art by Claudia Ianniciello

ISBN 13: 978-1-963517-03-3

First Edition: May, 2018
First Hardcover Edition, February 2024

For Glory

Also by Stuart Jaffe

Max Porter Paranormal Mysteries

Southern Bound
Southern Charm
Southern Belle
Southern Gothic
Southern Haunts
Southern Curses
Southern Rites
Southern Craft
Southern Spirit
Southern Flames
Southern Fury
Southern Souls
Southern Blood
Southern Graves
Southern Dead
Southern Hexes
Southern Hart

Nathan K Thrillers

Immortal Killers
Killing Machine
The Cardinal
Yukon Massacre
The First Battle
Immortal Darkness
A Spy for Eternity
Prisoner
Desert Takedown
Lone Star Standoff
The Puppeteer
Blowback
Prime

The Ridnight Mysteries

The Water Blade
The Waters of Taladoro
Waterfire

The Parallel Society

The Infinity Caverns
Book on the Isle
Rift Angel
Lost Time
Pages of Glass
The Bold Warrior
City of Infinity

The Malja Chronicles

The Way of the Black Beast
The Way of the Sword and Gun
The Way of the Brother Gods
The Way of the Blade
The Way of the Power
The Way of the Soul

Gillian Boone novels

A Glimpse of Her Soul
Pathway to Spirit

Stand Alone Novels

After The Crash
Real Magic
Founders

Short Story Collection

10 Bits of My Brain
10 More Bits of My Brain
The Bluesman
The Marshall Drummond Case Files: Cabinet 1
The Marshall Drummond Case Files: Cabinet 2
The Marshall Drummond Case Files: Cabinet 3

Non-Fiction

How to Write Magical Words: A Writer's Companion
For more information, please visit ***www.stuartjaffe.com***

Southern Flames

Chapter 1

STANDING IN THE BACK CORNER of his office, sandwiched between his mother and his ghost partner, Max Porter watched his wife hugging another man and wondered how the day had reached this point. Max's mother, a short but formidable woman, crossed her arms with a huff. Marshall Drummond, the ghost of a 1940s detective, clicked his tongue as he pulled down the front of his Fedora.

"Bad enough I have to watch you and her mooning over each other all the time," Drummond said, thrusting his pale hands into his trench coat. He flew across the room and into the built-in bookcase that he considered home. "I can't stomach watching her with another guy."

Though Mrs. Porter could not see or hear Drummond, she nodded in agreement. "It's just wrong to display that much affection. Especially in front of you."

Across the room, Sandra wiped tears from her eyes and wrapped her arms around the man once more. Chiseled face, broad chest, and over six feet tall — the man looked like an NFL quarterback in his prime. Compared to Max, the man's stature rose to the level of an Adonis.

But just that morning, Max had stood on the lawn of his Winston-Salem home and thought that overall their life had been looking up. Their house had been on the market for only a few weeks and already several buyers had showed interest. Once it eventually sold and they paid off the outstanding mortgage, the remaining profit would be more than enough to set them up comfortably somewhere else. Preferably a place where no one had burst into flames in the garage.

Since that horrible incident, Max and Sandra opted to park their cars in the driveway.

With a giggle, Sandra pulled away from the man. "I'm so sorry, honey," she said, reaching out towards Max. "I didn't mean to be rude, but this really caught me by surprise. I haven't seen this guy since high school."

The big man walked over and put out a large hand. "I'm Peter Rathburn. Pleasure to meet you."

Max shook the man's hand — he didn't want to, but he saw no sense in causing trouble. Not yet. "So, you know my wife from high school?"

Peter put his arm around Sandra and squeezed tight. "She was my girlfriend for two years. We even went to the prom together."

Max raised an eyebrow toward Sandra. "I don't think you ever mentioned dating a guy named Peter."

With an exuberant laugh, Peter said, "Really? You were the first girl I ever kissed, and I don't even earn a mention to your husband?"

"I guess it never came up." She lowered her head slightly and hurried over to the counter. Picking up a coffee mug, she poured a cup and offered it to Peter.

While standing on the lawn that morning, as Max considered options for their future, he had watched Sandra walk down the front steps with a mug of coffee for him. He thought so, at least. When she sidled up next to him, however, she only offered to share the caffeine booster. After taking a sip, he put his arm around her shoulder and held her tight.

She wore a silk bathrobe that he had bought for her when they first moved into this house — when they first had money that didn't have to go to food or heat. He kissed the top of her head. Her damp hair smelled of shampoo, and he had the idea of blowing off the day, sweeping her into his arms, and carrying her back into the house. The next several days would have been infinitely better, if he had listened to his little brain.

"Out with it," she said. "What's troubling you?"

Max chuckled. He had not recognized his thoughts as troubling. But she was right. Under the surface of dreams of the future, of imagining a new house, of thinking about making love, a dark reality simmered.

"Is it money?" she asked.

He shook his head. "Once we sell this, we'll have plenty again. That is, unless you insist we buy another big place."

She leaned her head on his chest. "We hardly have enough time to live in this one as it is."

The coffee smelled good, and he wanted another sip, but he didn't want her to move her head either.

"If not money, what is it?"

He didn't know how to answer at first. But as he opened his mouth, thoughts and words formed simultaneously. "It's the Magi. They've been very quiet lately."

"That's a bad thing? As far as I can see, no news is good news when it comes to them."

"We haven't heard a word from Mother Hope." Unconsciously, Max's hand reached up and rubbed his chest where Mother Hope had cursed him several years ago. She had yet to use the curse, but the threat followed him like a dark cloud. She also controlled the Magi. Supposedly, the group existed to protect the people from abusive witches, but reality had shown him that Mother Hope might be the worst witch of them all. "Not that I want to be drawn into any mess of hers, but at least when that happens, we know what's going on with her and the Magi. This silence is worse than any job she'd force us into."

Sandra said, "What about Leon? Since we pulled off that curse on him, I would've thought we might get some information from him."

With the help of the Mobley Coven, the most powerful coven in the Carolinas, Max had cursed Leon Moore. He was Mother Hope's right hand, and now, any magic she used against Max would hurt Leon as well.

"I promised he wouldn't have to spy for us," Max said. "He still knows I'll call in a favor or two when I need it, but I figured that would be dangerous enough. I also don't want him to realize that there are limits to what I can do with that linking curse. If he ever figures it out, he could cause major damage to both of us."

"And that's it? Just the usual bothering you?"

"Shouldn't it bother me that any of that is considered *the usual?*"

"It's the life we lead." She nestled closer to him. "Anything else on your mind?"

At that moment, Max did not have a good answer for her. But now, staring at Mr. Perfection in his office, he had plenty on his mind.

Mrs. Porter grabbed her coat and walked to the door. "Well, clearly you all have some catching up to do, but it's time for me to go pick up the boys." She shot a narrow glare at Sandra. "Unless you want to go pick up your sons?"

Peter's face broke into a joyful grin. "You have sons? That's wonderful. I bet they're just as stubborn as you always were. I'd love to meet them."

"They're rather new additions to our family," Sandra said. "We adopted them."

"That's not quite true," Mrs. Porter said. "They're not really adopted yet. You're still going through the process of becoming their legal guardians. In fact, it's probably better that I pick them up. We don't need anybody seeing you with an ex-lover."

Before Sandra could respond, Mrs. Porter went out the door. Normally, Max hated when his mother sniped at his wife. But he had to admit a part of him — a childish part — jumped high in the air and whooped for his mother's sharp tongue.

To cover the awkward silence that had formed, Sandra sat at her desk and said, "So, I don't think you're here just to reminisce on old times. I saw the look on your face when you walked in here — you weren't expecting to find me. So, what's up? Is there something we can do for you?"

All of Peter's joy vanished with his smile. "Yeah. I mean, you guys are the ones who look into the odd cases, right? Like the weird ones? You know what I'm saying?"

"You've got a problem with a ghost."

"I think so."

Sitting at his desk, Max sighed. "Okay. Tell us about it."

Drummond poked his head out of the bookcase. “Well, damn, I guess I’ll have to listen to this clown, too.”

Chapter 2

DESPITE HIS TESTOSTERONE-LADEN APPEARANCE, Peter faltered as he settled into a chair opposite Sandra. The petty side of Max inwardly grinned. Leaning back, Max popped his feet on his desk. "Okay, Mr. Rathburn, let's hear it."

Peter's smile took on a plastic appearance, but Max could see the tremors underneath. He'd seen enough fear in the eyes of clients to recognize it now. Sandra did, too.

Leaning across the desk, she said, "It's okay. We've seen a lot of weird things. Trust me. Anything you want to share, we won't judge."

Drummond flicked the brim of his hat. "Speak for yourself, doll."

"She's right," Max said, though he'd rather be like Drummond for the moment — able to speak his mind without being heard. "Tell us your story. Don't leave anything out. People always leave stuff out and it only makes it worse in the end. You can trust us. Heck, she's your old girlfriend. Trust her."

With a bashful scratch behind his ear, Peter said, "I guess it doesn't make much sense for me to have come this whole way and not tell you what's going on. I just didn't think it would be so hard when the moment came."

Sandra kept her focus on Peter — probably to help ease Peter's mind, but also to ignore Max and Drummond's comments. "Start whenever you're ready. Go as far back as you want. We're here to listen."

"Great," Drummond said. "Are we going to have to hear about your high school prom again? I might have better things to do."

Sandra tilted her head towards the ghost and raised an

eyebrow.

"Okay, okay. I don't have anything better to do. Still —"

Peter cleared his throat, sniffled, and took a deep breath. "I'm a firefighter. Been one since my college days. Sophomore year — some guys convinced me to try volunteering for the EMTs. I loved it. Did that all the way through graduation, and that led to joining the fire department. Started out in Virginia, worked in Richmond for several years, and then got a job down in Raleigh. That's where I've been for the last ten years or so. But then an opportunity popped up to move out here, so I took it."

"How long have you been here?" Max asked.

"Not long. Why?"

"I was wondering why you hadn't reached out to Sandra until now." Max knew it was a meek jibe, but he would take whatever breadcrumbs he could find.

"Like she said, I had no idea she was here. Not until yesterday. But everything started weeks ago."

Throwing Max a sharp look, Sandra said, "Forgive us. We don't need to keep interrupting. Please, continue."

"Well, it started with some small sounds. I guess that's how these things usually start. At least, that's the way it is in the movies. Nothing really scary — just odd noises in the walls at night. Several of the other firefighters made jokes about it being a ghost. I didn't think much of it. Most every firehouse has some sort of ghost story behind it, and newbies often get teased with such things. Consider it harmless hazing.

"I guess the first time it became something serious was when we got a call for an apartment fire. There's a rec room for us to hang out in — TV, video games, ping-pong tables, that kind of thing — and when the call came in, I rushed out into the hall to go to the garage and get my equipment. One of the other guys, Owen, came up behind me, but the rec room door slammed shut. He couldn't get it open. Several of us on the other side rammed against the door, but it wouldn't budge. We were punching that thing and kicking and Mackenzie even got a crowbar, but nothing worked. We had no choice. Every second we waited, that fire was burning. Owen knew it, too. He waved us on, and we rushed to the engine to head off."

Max sat forward. "And Owen?"

"When we got back, he was fine. Sitting in the kitchen, eating a sandwich. He said once we left, the door opened by itself.

"I thought the whole door thing was an elaborate prank for me. But no matter how many times I brought it up, everybody insisted it was not a planned joke. And one look at Owen convinced me they were telling the truth. He looked petrified.

"After that, things started to intensify. Everybody noticed personal items missing. Things would just vanish, but we couldn't find any evidence of a thief or break-in or anything. And then right at the point where people would start yelling at each other, somebody would find the missing item, and it would always be in an unusual, unlikely place. Like Beth — she had this snow globe from her only trip to New York City. Kept it with her whenever she was putting in her hours at the firehouse. Everybody knew it was hers, and she always had it next to her bunk. But then one afternoon she saw it was gone. All of us in the house helped her search, but nobody could find it. Then, when I could hear in her voice that the anger was hitting the boiling point, Captain Renner found it balanced on top of the bulletin board in the hallway.

"You understand? Every single one of us had to have gone right by that bulletin board a million times in our search. There is no way all of us could have missed it. It's just not possible."

"And this brought you here?" Max asked.

"There's more. Wishing that'd be enough?"

Sandra said, "What my husband means is that most people who come to us because of this kind of thing don't come after a few disturbances. Things have to get really bad before they're willing to entertain the idea of finding somebody like us."

Peter squirmed in his chair. "Things got a lot worse. It got to the point where every call that came in was accompanied by missing equipment or the locked rec room door or even one time, all the power went out in the middle of the night. Nobody would do anything about it. Mostly because Captain Renner refused to believe in the possibility that it might be a ghost. He always had some way to dismiss things — rusty hinges, bad wiring, you name it. But I remembered back in high school. You talked about ghosts a lot."

"I did?"

"Sure. I could tell even then that you were dealing with something, but I was too young to know what. Later in my life, whenever I thought about you —"

"You thought about me?" Sandra blushed.

With a charismatic wink, Peter said, "No guy could forget a girl like you."

As calmly as he could manage, which did not go far enough, Max said, "Can we get back to your story?"

Losing all his charm, Peter went on. "Well, the more I thought about you, the more I saw that you probably saw ghosts. I've met a few other people like that. People I trusted. So, I figured if the captain won't do anything about it and everybody else was too scared, I could do something."

Max grabbed a pen and tapped it against the table. "So you called us?"

"Not at first. I called a psychic."

Drummond snorted. "This keeps getting better and better. Big, tough square jaw here called in a fortuneteller."

"I know what you're thinking," Peter said, flashing some renewed charm at Sandra. "What kind of crackpot did I bring into the firehouse? But, like I said, I have friends who can see ghosts. I trust them and they recommended this woman — Irene Beck."

Max pulled his notebook from the desk drawer. He flipped to a blank page and wrote down the name — *Irene Beck*. "What happened when the psychic showed up?"

"She came by one afternoon. I met her outside and escorted her down the hall to the kitchen, but we never made it that far. She started shaking. I thought she was having a seizure, but before I could do anything, before I could even yell out for someone to call an ambulance, the shaking stopped. She turned to leave but I begged her to at least take a look at the rec room. I guilted her into it, really. I reminded her that we're firefighters. We save lives. We can't go on like this. Against her better judgment, she followed me further down the hall. When I opened the rec room door, she froze in place, her eyes got real big, and she let out a scream as if she were on fire. She ran back down the hall and out to her car. By the time I got to the parking lot, she had already driven half-a-block away.

"She called me the next day. Apologized and told me that I needed some serious help. A specialist. She suggested I find a ghost hunter-type-person. So, I searched the internet and found your website. When I saw the picture of Sandra, I recognized you right away. I took it as a sign. That's why I came here. But I was still shocked when I walked in and saw you for real. I think part of me had convinced the rest of me you'd be some other Sandra who only looked like the Sandra I knew."

Max did not need to look at Sandra to know she wanted to take the case. He didn't need to look at Drummond, either. That old ghost would think that a prankster haunting was beneath him. He liked to deal with murder cases and other such challenges. Which meant that Max had the deciding vote.

Not really, though. Denying the case meant hurting Sandra, and he would not do that. "I guess we could take a few hours to check out the firehouse. See if there's a case there or not."

"Really?" Peter said.

"Really?" Drummond said.

Sandra smiled. "Really."

Chapter 3

THE FIREHOUSE WAS LOCATED in the northeastern part of the city. Though only a short drive from their office, Sandra decided to drive with Peter and have Max follow behind. She only wanted to spend some extra time with her high school friend and reminisce about old times. Max agreed — old friends like to reminisce. His grip on the steering wheel betrayed other, darker thoughts.

It didn't help that Drummond appeared in the passenger seat and said, "I can't believe you're okay with any of this. They were dating. They were kissing."

"They were in high school. Almost two decades ago. Besides, I'm the one who married her. So there's nothing to be threatened about."

"Sure. No reason to fear a guy whose looks would make Gary Cooper feel puny."

"You're not helping." Max wanted to punch Drummond in the arm, but the chill that came from passing through a ghost would be unpleasant enough — and should Drummond decide to hit back, the icy pain from being touched by a ghost dissuaded him completely.

As they approached the firehouse, Max weaved around a few large potholes. On his left, train tracks paralleled the road, and about a quarter-mile further up, they opened into a freight yard. The highway passed overhead and graffiti painted the sidewalks nearby.

Peter led them around to a parking lot in the back. From the outside, the place looked like a suburban home complete with the grassy front yard, well-trimmed walkway up to the front door, and a small overhang porch. The only giveaway that this was a firehouse, and it was a big giveaway, was the oversized garage that housed the two red engines.

As everyone exited the cars, Peter walked ahead like a giddy schoolboy. They entered through the back of the garage, its massive bay doors were both open, and Max had to admit that he felt a little bit of his inner-schoolboy awaken. Seeing those two large fire trucks brought back memories of playing on the kitchen floor with toy cars while wearing a firefighter's helmet.

But joy vanished as he felt an unusual tension in the air.

A hearty woman sat in an old used office chair. Behind her, papers cluttered a dented, metal desk. On the opposite side of the garage, Max noticed two soda machines and all the open locker bays filled with firefighting equipment.

"You the woo-woo people?" the woman said, wiggling her fingers at the side of her head.

With a nervous laugh, Peter said, "Everybody, this is Stacy. She's one of our female firefighters. And she also thinks this is all nonsense."

Max winked at Stacy. "I'm hoping it's all nonsense, too."

While Stacy kept her eye on them, Peter led the way inside. Walking backwards like a tour guide, he said, "Let me show you around, so you can see if you feel anything."

Max glanced behind at Drummond. Floating through the wall, Drummond said, "I know, I know. I'll go check out the whole place while you guys take the grand tour."

Max caught up to his wife and spotted the slight grin on her face. He assumed that she smiled at Drummond's usual antics, yet she kept her eyes forward on Peter. Max wanted to put his hand around her waist, but the main hall of the firehouse did not give them enough room to do so.

While the outside of the firehouse looked like a well-manicured suburban home that had been plunked down in an urban rail district, the inside had been institutionalized much like a modern college dorm. Cinderblock walls had been painted pale yellow and florescent lights had been mounted to the ceiling. On one side of the hall, a map of Winston-Salem had been framed with all the districts marked in different colors denoting which firehouse was responsible for which areas.

They walked by an open door with a nameplate reading *Capt. Renner*. Glancing inside, Max saw a large dorm room — thin office carpeting, a single bed, and a desk with a small bookshelf. Drab colors all around. One window offered meager light. Further on, they saw another dorm room. This one had been set up for two, and the window had been covered with a thick, black sheet.

"Sometimes the only sleep we get is during the day," Peter explained.

Sandra's eyes roved around the room and Max could read her expression — clean enough, but she thought the room needed a feminine touch. Then she squinted. Max leaned close to ask her if she saw something, but she shook her head before he spoke.

"I'd like to see the rec room," she said. "That's where the majority of the disturbances have happened, right?"

Peter swallowed hard. "It's right up this way, just before the kitchen."

From the dorm room across the hall, a loud voice called, "Hey Petey, looks like you rassled up some more suckers for your ghost hunt."

Deflated, Peter gestured to two burly men, both bald with wide grins. They each wore a gray T-shirt bearing the fire department logo and sweatpants with the same. The one who had called out wore sunglasses backwards on his head.

"This is Owen and Chuck Williams. Guys, these are the people from the Porter Agency. And yes, they're here to check things out."

The brothers chuckled. Owen folded his arms and leaned back in his chair. "This is all a waste of time, you know. We got a door that gets stuck real easy and a bunch of superstitious idiots scaring themselves at night."

Stretched out on one of the beds, Chuck snorted a laugh. "Don't forget that the ghost likes to steal things, too. Even took your underwear."

"That was you."

Chuck rolled his head on the pillow and laughed heartily. "I thought I fooled you with that one."

Owen rolled his eyes. "What would a ghost want with my dirty underwear?"

"Ask Peter. It's his ghost."

"Is that right, Petey? Does your ghost like my underwear?"

Peter leaned his shoulder against the doorjamb. "Keep laughing. Next time I make dinner, I'll make you pork chops." That wiped the smile from the man's face. As an aside towards Max and Sandra, Peter added, "Pork chops for dinner brings on a fire that night. It's just one of about a million little superstitions firefighters have."

"Hey," Owen said, tilting his chin up. "We may have our good and bad luck charms, but at least we don't believe in ghosts haunting the firehouse."

Max did not quite believe them. They seemed overenthusiastic to tease Peter and overly dismissive of the mounting evidence that something wrong was going on here. They seemed nervous.

"Rathburn." The voice came from down the hall.

Peter spun around. "Yes sir."

Captain Renner stepped into the hall from the kitchen at the end. He was a dark black man with sharp cheekbones and the build of a linebacker. "Who are all these people clogging up the way?"

"Sorry, sir. These are the people with the Porter Agency."

From the dorm room, Owen yelled, "They're the psychics, Cap."

The Captain's curled lip contained an inferno of disdain for psychics. "I see. And what is it you hope to achieve by being here? Besides helping out Peter with his problem?"

Max snickered. While the captain formed an imposing figure, he had no idea what he was up against with Sandra Porter. She marched straight up to the man and never flinched. "We're not some circus show here to amuse you. We're not publicity hounds looking to get our pictures in the papers or to land a TV deal on some small network. We're not charlatans. We are the real deal, and we're here to help. But if that help is not wanted or appreciated, we've got better things to do than waste our days being insulted."

The captain took a step back. "I'm sorry, ma'am. I did not mean to be rude. It's just that we've had so-called psychics in here before. The last one made such a scene that it was more upsetting than if she had not been here to begin with."

Max stepped forward. "Was that Irene Beck?"

"I don't recall her name. Peter? Was that her?"

Peter nodded.

A loudspeaker burst out two long tones. All the firefighters perked up and listened close. Though Max knew the words spoken were in English, he could not decipher the blaring sounds — loud enough to wake even the deepest sleeper. When the dispatch voice finished, Captain Renner hurried down the hall.

"Chuck, Beth, Stacy — with me."

Chuck jumped to his feet and barreled into the hall. A woman stepped out from a side door — presumably Beth — and followed toward the garage. Watching them rush off to suit up and jump into the fire engine, Max felt excitement course throughout his bones. He saw Stacy hustling around in the garage, and he glanced at Peter. "You don't all have to go fight the fire?"

Peter walked toward the kitchen. "They're not off to fight a fire. Fire departments in just about every place in the country are the catchall for when the 9-1-1 dispatchers don't know where to send a call."

"That makes a lot more sense," Sandra said. "I swore I heard her say there was a child with his head caught."

"Kids with their heads in banisters, cats up trees, medical emergencies that should go to EMTs or an ambulance, car accidents, you name it. Most days, we don't fight that many fires. Unless you're in a massive city, you get plenty of days without a single fire. The worst is when we're off doing one of these BS calls and we're not able to get to a real fire as soon as we should."

As the engine pulled out of the garage, Drummond flew up

the hallway. "I've been all over this building, even checked the attic and beneath the ground — I got nothing. If there's a ghost haunting this building, it's a ghost of a ghost because otherwise I should be seeing it."

Placing her hand on Peter's muscular bicep, Sandra said, "I'm sorry, but I'm not seeing anything here."

Owen poked his head out of his room. "Told you that psychic was a crock. She was all song and dance."

Peter looked straight at Sandra. "I'm not making this up."

"I'm not saying you are, but I can't see anything. I don't feel anything. I'm getting no sense that this place is haunted."

"At least come see the rec room. That's where most everything happens. It's just up ahead. The door on the left right before the kitchen."

Sandra looked back at Max. He shrugged. They had come all this way — might as well finish their tour. They walked down the remainder of the hall, and when they reached the door leading into the rec room, Max's chest tightened.

The spot where Mother Hope had cursed him ignited with a painful burn. He grabbed his chest with one hand and steadied himself against the wall with the other. Sandra gasped as her hands went to her head. She clenched her eyes shut and stumbled forward.

Max thought he might throw up. He tried to speak but his throat had constricted to the point that even breathing strained his muscles. Like a voice calling from a far-off distance, he heard Peter say, "Owen, get over here. I need help."

Thick hands took hold of Max's shoulders and guided him forward. Up ahead, Max saw Peter carrying Sandra into the kitchen at the end of the hall. Seconds later, Max found himself sitting at a long kitchen table while two pale and frightened firefighters poured glasses of water for everybody.

"What was that?" Peter asked, the water in his glass shaking over the edges.

Max could not form words yet. He gazed around the large kitchen. An L-shaped counter ran across two walls. A refrigerator had been parked at one end of the counter while a second refrigerator stood alone against one of the bare walls. The sink was clean, and the counter well-organized. Whoever had the job of maintaining the kitchen took their work seriously.

Sandra drank half a glass of water. "I'm okay now. Something hit me in the head, though. Like an instant migraine." Putting out her hand towards Max, she added, "You okay?"

Max reached across. The mere act of lacing his fingers with hers eased his rapid beating hard. "Had some chest pains, that's all."

Owen rushed over to Max's side. "Have you ever had a heart attack? Any history of heart attack in your family?"

Waving him off, Max said, "No, no. Nothing like that. It wasn't a heart attack. It was the kind of chest pains you can get when encountering those things you don't seem to want to believe in."

Drummond floated by the hall door. "I swear I didn't see anything, I didn't feel anything, when I searched." He gazed down the long hallway and his voice darkened. "This is a serious one, isn't it?"

Max gave a slight nod.

"Okay," Sandra said. "We've seen enough. We'll take the case."

Owen had no snappy reply.

Chapter 4

MAX AND DRUMMOND SPED WEST along Route 40 towards the Louisville-Clemmons exit. Earlier, after touring the firehouse, they all had returned to the office to discuss how to move forward. First, however, Sandra gobbled down five ibuprofen while Max drank from the whiskey flask Drummond kept hidden in a hollowed book.

Drummond pursed his lips as he floated around the office ceiling. "I've been involved with a lot of strange cases, but I can't recall ever taking one on that had nobody to investigate. I mean, I know there's a victim — clearly the two of you were attacked by something — but I didn't see a ghost. Even if I had, we don't have a name or even a time period that this ghost comes from. Which can't be a ghost because I'm a ghost and I'm telling you, we don't behave like that."

Placing the whiskey flask back in the book, Max said, "We do have one name — Peter Rathburn. Maybe we should start with him."

Sandra rubbed her temples. "Stop acting like you're in high school."

"All I meant was —"

"I know exactly what you meant." Before things could escalate, she grabbed her keys and coat. "I am going to look into why we can't see or hear or even talk to this ghost."

"Not a ghost," Drummond said.

"Whatever it is. I've got the contacts, so that's what I'm going to do."

"It's a good idea, doll. As for us, I know exactly where we need to go."

As Max turned left off the exit ramp, he had to admit that Drummond was right. Other than themselves, the only person they could talk to who might be able to provide more information was the psychic hired by the firefighters — Irene Beck. They found her address with ease. She ran a small business selling *Unusual Items Touched By The Supernatural!*

The area around the Louisville-Clemmons exit had built up with restaurants, strip malls, supermarkets, and banks. But after a mile, old starter homes now converted to small businesses dotted the landscape. One of these homes bore a large white sign with a large pink hand emblazoned with a large eye centered on the palm. The word PSYCHIC curved above.

"You know, after dealing with witches, ghosts, and people of real power," Drummond said as they pulled in the driveway, "this feels like a step down."

"You'd rather I set up a meeting with Mother Hope? I'm sure she has some unique and special ways to torture a ghost."

Drummond cocked his head to the side as if in deep thought. "Starting to see the value of Irene Beck. I think there's a lot of important information we could probably get from her."

As cars whizzed by on the busy, main stretch, Max walked up to the front door. A handwritten sign had been taped about head height. It read: *We're open. Come on in.* Inside, Max found what had probably been a lovely home at one time. Small but functional. A good first investment for a young couple. But now, the place had been geared toward sales.

The living room had been converted into the main show floor. Spinning racks displayed books on the occult, fortune-telling, and all manner of New Age psychic healing. A glass display counter offered up numerous gems labelled with cards that informed of the various magical properties in each stone. The far wall sold everything from incense to tarot cards to Ouija boards. Music piping in through corner speakers filled the room with the deep droning tones of Taoist monks.

Passing through a beaded curtain that revealed a dirty kitchen, a middle-aged woman entered the room. "My oh my, I don't usually get such a good looking gentleman entering my establishment. I am Irene Beck." She was a small woman with a big voice and a long, Southern drawl. Though heavyset, she moved with confidence and charm.

Max liked this woman. He did not relish where this conversation would most likely go. At least, there were no other patrons in the room. He'd hate to embarrass this woman, possibly call her a fraud, in front of a customer.

Drummond hovered before a display of handmade, wooden necklaces. A sign above read *Ghost and Spirit Wards*. He poked his finger through the necklaces. "At least we don't have to worry about her being a witch."

Max chuckled.

Irene settled behind the long glass counter and presented a venomous smile. "Something amusing you?"

Leaning an elbow on the counter, he said, "Shouldn't you be able to tell me what I'm thinking?"

Irene took one step back and crossed her arms. She stared at Max for a moment and then her gaze drifted toward the display of ghost wards. "Don't let all the little knickknacks fool you. I'm quite the real deal, honey. I don't know why you're here, but I know for sure you're not here to buy any of this crap. You here to cause a sweet, kind lady like me trouble? Or do you want a reading? Or is it something else?"

Drummond stared back with his mouth open. "Lady, can you hear me? You see me?"

Irene did not respond. But after a moment of silence, her face wrinkled as she narrowed her gaze in Drummond's direction. "I'm guessing there's a ghost in this room. Is he or she sayin' something to me?"

"I don't understand," Max said. "You can sense there's a ghost in here but you can't tell what he's saying?"

"I don't like tests, sir. And I don't do parlor tricks. If I take the time, I'm sure I could tune into your friend here and find out what's going on, but it's clear to me that you are not afraid of this ghost and that you are not here because of him. What I don't know is why you are here. Care to help a girl out?"

"I'm Max Porter. I'm here because —"

"Oh, I see. The Porter Agency. You have quite the

reputation in some circles."

"Really? I didn't think anybody knew we existed."

"Oh honey, the world I live in is not that big. People talk. And you've done enough shaking up around this town that I was bound to hear."

"I don't know whether to be flattered or scared. I think I'll go with flattered for the time being."

Irene laughed and pointed a manicured fingernail at Max. "You and I are going to get along just fine. So, Max of the Porter Agency, how can I help you?"

"We've been hired to investigate some unnatural activities going on at one of the firehouses. They told us you had been there before us."

Irene's pleasant countenance dropped like a stone in a cold river. "I see you don't mess around."

"I'm sorry if this upsets you, but it would be very helpful if you could share with me what happened."

"Don't you ask me to go back. I will not do it."

Keeping a calm tone, Max said, "We're staying right here. Just talking."

Her right eye twitched and her thumbs rubbed her fingertips. "That thing. That is not … No. It's not a ghost. Not a spirit. It's something else, something I don't ever want to feel again. It's lost. Confused. It runs around in my head, going in circles, never stopping."

Drummond said, "I think meeting that ghost stirred up her brains a bit."

Irene paced the length of the counter like a trapped animal. "No, no, no. It's all wrong in there. A broken spirit. That's what I felt. But not a spirit at all. It's a nothing. I mean, it's something, that it is, but nothing like I've ever experienced before. And I don't want to see it again."

Putting on his best smile, Max said, "All I need is a name. That thing you felt, it had to have once been a person. What's the person's name?"

"I don't know if it ever was a person. Maybe it's a demon. You believe in demons?"

Drummond said, "If she's about to go spout Angels and Demons, we'll never get anywhere."

She paused and wagged that fingernail at Max again. "I can see you are not a religious man. You should be. Strong beliefs are what separate us from the animals."

"That may be so," Max said, "but for now, I just need that name. You know the name. I can see it in your eyes." He could see no such thing, but her reticence convinced him to bluff.

Her eyes darted around the room before settling back on Max's face. With a quiver in her voice, she said, "I want to help you. I do. You seem like a nice man, but if I tell you, then it will come back to haunt me."

"From everything I've heard, this thing is staying at the firehouse."

"No, honey. I don't mean that thing. I mean the fact that I gave up a name — it'll get out. There are people in this town who will not like me helping you."

Max stepped back and put out his hands in an open gesture. "We all have to choose sides sometimes."

"Enough of this," Drummond said. He slipped over to one of the book racks, gritted his teeth, and shoved the rack over. Physical contact with the corporal world caused a ghost serious pain. Drummond yelled, clasping his hand as if he had touched a burning stove.

Max did not have to explain to Irene what had happened. Her wide-eyed stare told him that she understood everything. Shifting from an easy-going charm to a stern, authoritative tone, he said, "Don't make this worse. Give me the name and I swear I will keep you out of it. Nobody will ever know that you told us anything."

"I don't know," she said, inching toward the beaded curtain.

"Give me the name, and you'll never see me again."

If she ran, Max did not know what he would do. The idea of chasing down this lady, tackling her, and forcing her to reveal the name seemed ludicrous. But he couldn't leave empty-handed, either. Thankfully, she solved his dilemma.

"Holly Claypool," she sputtered. "That's the name — Holly

Claypool. Now get out of here."

Without waiting to see if they followed her commands, she rushed through the beaded curtain. As she stomped up an unseen stairway, Max and Drummond headed out to the car. Once they were back on the highway, Max said, "I want you to go ahead and check on Sandra. See if you can help her. If she needs anything from me, let me know."

"You got it," Drummond said. "I can see I'm not going to want to hang out with you for the next few hours anyway. We've got a name now. I'm guessing you're headed to the library to do what you're good at — research."

"Sorry that we can't all be good at terrorizing middle-aged women."

"Hey, I got her to give up the name, didn't I?"

"You didn't have to threaten her. I was doing fine. A few more minutes and she would have told me just as easily."

"My way guaranteed the result. You still have plenty to learn from me, so don't start thinking you know it all."

"That's not what I was suggesting, and you know it."

"Interrogation takes years of practice and learning. It's not just looking up names in a search engine. Heck, I'm sure I could go to the library and find out all about Holly Claypool."

"Are you volunteering to do the research instead?"

"Not on your life."

Max chuckled. "Didn't think so."

Chapter 5

RESEARCH PROVED EASY. Within an hour, Max had uncovered the story of Holly Claypool including the names and addresses of several people involved that were still alive. Evening approached as he returned home to find that his mother had already dropped off PB and J. Sandra fed them dinner and listened to their stories of school.

Jammer J, the younger of the two, spoke enthusiastically of his teachers, his subjects, and even the few acquaintances he had. Sandra worried that the boy had difficulty making real friends, anything beyond a casual school friend, but Max pointed out that PB and J both had spent so much time homeless, relying only on each other, that learning to trust other kids their age would take time. PB, on the other hand, spent most of his days homeschooled by Max's mother. In order for Mrs. Porter to have some privacy and some sanity, PB often took extra courses through the YMCA, the Homeschooling Association, and other outreach programs. He spent most of his time talking about the other kids — classes bored him. While not exactly friends, these kids tended to be more than what J could muster in others. PB had that charisma which ingratiated him to people.

After they ate, Sandra ordered the boys upstairs to wash up and get ready for bed. They didn't really have a bedtime — after all, as best as anybody could figure out, they were barely teenagers — but Sandra had learned that the boys responded well to some parental structure. Plus, they appeared to enjoy spending the night more and more. As Max and Sandra navigated their way through the paperwork of becoming guardians, they eased the boys into the idea of living together under one roof. Though PB was the most reticent about giving up his apartment, with every sleepover, they became more amenable.

Max sat at his desk in his study to review his notes. He would miss this study. Of all the rooms in the house, this one had meant the most to him. But he had a straight view through the door across the kitchen and to the door leading into the garage — where he witnessed a cursed man combust. Just glancing in the direction of the garage brought back those tortured memories of watching that man burn.

Before his brain could remind him of the acrid odor, Drummond slipped in through the wall. "I was waiting at the office for you guys to show up, but since that wasn't happening, I'm here. Tell me what you learned."

"Not yet. We'll wait for Sandra and the Sandwich Boys to finish up."

Less than ten minutes later, they all adjourned to the living room. Sandra and Max settled on the couch while the boys spread out on the carpeted floor. Drummond opted to float in a seated position by the ottoman.

PB had a small bowl of chocolate covered raisins, and he popped one in his mouth. "Is this a new case or are you just sharing with us some obscure, boring little story you found somewhere?"

"Boring?" Max said. "My stories are never boring."

J giggled and even Sandra cracked a smile. Rubbing Max's arm, she said, "No, honey, never boring. Though sometimes more detailed than we need."

"I'll say," Drummond chimed in.

Max overacted rolling his eyes. Turning serious, he said to the boys, "Pay attention, this is for a case. We're investigating the death of a woman named Holly Claypool. She was murdered in 1973."

J leaned towards PB. "This'll be good. The murder stories are always the best."

Sandra snapped her fingers. "Okay, time to calm down. If you two yap the whole way through, he's just going to have to tell the story all over again."

Max's mouth turned down. "You all are filling me with such confidence."

"We tease because we love." She pecked him on the cheek.

Drummond swiped his hat off and placed it on his knee. "Are you going to get to this story or do I have to sit here and watch you two be mushy? I'm happy you love each other, but I don't need to see it all the time."

Max scooted to the edge of the couch and rested his elbows on his knees. On the coffee table, he placed a yellow folder. He cleared his throat and focused on the story he had to share.

"In 1971, there was a nineteen-year-old girl named Holly Claypool. Born and raised here in Winston-Salem, she lived with her brother in a townhouse on Granville Drive near Piedmont University. Her brother, Floyd, was three years older. He worked for R.J. Reynolds Tobacco downtown in the warehouses. Some kind of childhood accident had messed up his leg — I couldn't find the details on that — but the result was that he limped. Couple that with the fact that he was Holly's guardian, and there was no chance Floyd would be going to Vietnam."

From his folder, Max pulled out a picture of Holly Claypool that he had printed off the internet. The image came from her high school yearbook and showed a vibrant, young woman with straight blonde hair, parted in the middle, and a hopeful smile. He then pulled out a second photograph — this one of a young man with brown, shoulder-length hair that curled at the ends. He looked strong and athletic. The kind of guy that might be voted Most Popular.

As they passed around the picture, Max continued, "That's Wade Johnson. They met during their senior year, fell in love, and promised to get married when Wade returned from the war."

Sandra frowned. "The government didn't draft kids who were still in high school. Unless ... are you saying this guy volunteered?"

"That's right. According to the news reports, he had an adventurous streak — a bit of a violent one at that. Nobody was surprised that he wanted to go fighting a war."

The Sandwich Boys stayed quiet as they studied the photos. Max made a mental note to complement his mother. A year ago, these boys would have been peppering him with impatient questions. But after only a short time of academics, they had learned to listen closely, pay attention, and learn. Only when the entire lesson had finished would they ask things. Impressive.

"He spent a year-and-a-half in Vietnam," Max went on. "He would've stayed longer, but he took a bullet in the hip. Once that healed, it made it difficult for him to walk without pain. When he came back to Winston-Salem, the newspapers wrote a big article on him and many of the townsfolk came out to wish him well. But of course many more did not greet him with open arms. Coming back from Vietnam was not a cause for celebration among many. What little I could figure out about him from the articles, though, made me think none of that mattered to him. He never joined up for the honors but rather out of a sense of adventure and maybe duty."

Drummond said, "Let me guess — sweet gal Holly Claypool found another guy and shell-shocked Wade snapped. Poor bastard found out and killed her."

Max wanted to answer Drummond directly, but the boys still did not believe he spoke with a ghost. Better to avoid feeding into the idea that he might be crazy. Instead, he lowered his voice to pull them deeper into his tale. "Here's where things start to get strange."

The boys perked up.

"Holly had stayed true to Wade. She showered him with love and devotion. She understood that his transition back to civilian life would be difficult and showed every indication that she was up to the task of helping him through it. I even found a wedding announcement set for less than a month from the date that she died.

"According to the police, as reported in the newspapers, Wade met Holly in his apartment laundry room. She arrived first, wearing a paisley dress. Along the way, she had picked a few daisies and put them in her hair. She must have been so excited to see him — the wedding had her head filled with all the potential of their future. But when he showed up, I'm sure she sensed something was off. Her first thoughts were most likely related to Vietnam. Perhaps Wade was having a bad moment. She rushes over to him, whispers soothing words, but he's agitated, can't stop pacing around. He's building up his courage. Then with the speed and viciousness of a trained soldier, he throws her to the ground and wraps his fingers around her neck. She struggles, but he is too strong and she is too scared, too unprepared for the attack. He strangles her to death. Then he pulls a gun out of his pocket and shoots himself in the head."

"Huh?" PB said. "This guy has a gun all along and he takes the time to strangle this woman? Don't make no sense."

Max pulled out one final photograph from the folder. "It gets weirder. This is a copy of the photo they ran in the newspaper."

He handed the photo around. Though grainy and in black-and-white, it clearly depicted the crime scene. The two slumped bodies were a few feet apart — Wade against a dryer, Holly against the opposite wall. Blood splatter marred the walls behind them both. Dark blood pooled on the floor and mingled with the shadows of police officers standing around.

Max watched Sandra's face. The moment she saw it, he knew. Though the lines were faint and possibly brushed out of the photographs, it was clear that somebody had drawn a casting circle on the floor.

She bit her bottom lip. "Oh, crap."

Chapter 6

THE NEXT MORNING EVERYBODY ROSE EARLY to get cracking on their assignments. Sandra had come up empty the day before, but she planned to visit a lady who sold authentic occult ingredients to authentic witches. If this lady couldn't tell Sandra what kind of ghost-type thing they faced, then nobody would have the answer — that is, nobody the Porters wanted to deal with. They had no doubt there were plenty of witches with the answer, but those people would charge a deadly price for their help. Even a budding talent like Sandra would not be exempt from such deals.

Since it was Saturday, Sandra decided to take PB and J along with her. She pointed out that, after all, they needed to get used to being all together. "That's a big part of being a family, isn't it? Learning to live with each other."

Max took the hint. He needed to give some thought as to what kind of activities he could plan with the boys. Being their guardians had to mean more than simply paying for food and a roof. Max and Sandra cared about these boys, and they needed to learn how to show it. In the meantime, Max had a job to do.

The obvious first step would have been to drive out to the apartment building, inspect the laundry room, and see what they found. Unfortunately, the owners had difficulty keeping tenants after the murder-suicide. They tried to sell the building but found no takers. Eventually, they plowed down the structure and sold off the land. All that remained of the crime scene were the photographs.

In the newspaper articles surrounding the murder, however, the name Joe Pardini came up several times. He had served with Wade Johnson in Vietnam, and the two became friends through the common bond of having grown up in Winston-

Salem. Nearing seventy years old, Joe resided in an assisted living facility in Greensboro.

Max called him that morning, and after the initial shock wore off, Joe agreed to an interview. Drummond joined Max, and the two drove out.

As they neared the city, Drummond broke a pleasant silence. "Setting aside my ribbing of you, I want to make sure you're okay."

"Why wouldn't I be okay?"

"It might have something to do with your wife's ex-boyfriend who happens to be a handsome, well-built, firefighter. The guy goes around saving people's lives, for crying out loud."

"He could be Brad Pitt in his prime — doesn't matter. It's not about him. It's about how much I trust my wife, and I trust her a lot."

"First, I don't know who Brad Pitt is. Second, I'm not questioning your wife's loyalty. Sandra is one of the greatest gals I've ever met. That's not the point. A guy like Peter Rathburn can cause you all kinds of trouble. He's not going to turn Sandra's love away from you, steal her in the night, and make off with her for some whirlwind romance. That's not going to happen. You know it as well as I do. But, he can get her thinking."

Max gestured ahead toward the city. "I've got to go question this guy in a few minutes. Maybe you should be quiet and let me prepare."

Drummond swiveled wide so that his body poked out of the hood and he looked at Max head on. "You know how to question people just fine. It was probably the first thing I ever taught you. You're just trying to avoid this conversation."

"Get back in the passenger seat. You'll make me crash floating around in front of me like that."

As Drummond drifted back to his seat, he said, "I'm not trying to piss you off. I only want to help you avoid real problems down the road. Because that's what you're going to have if you ignore this."

"I'm not —"

"Rathburn is going to be talking to your wife. He's showing up and stirring around all these old memories. That's going to bring with it an emotion. You got that? An emotion that can burrow under the solid foundation that you and your wife have. She's not going to go leave you for him, but she is going to start comparing your relationship to this idealized, romanticized thing that she once had."

"She's not like that."

"The best dolls never are. Until they are."

Max pulled off the highway and drove along Friendly Avenue, then cut south toward Meadowood Street. In a few minutes, he would reach the Heritage Greens home, but he couldn't get there fast enough. "Are you done casting aspersions on my wife's character?"

Drummond scowled. "Don't act like I don't care about her. Only reason I'm saying any of this is because I don't want to see the two of you have problems."

"Fine. You love us both."

"I love her. Jury's still out about you."

"Okay. You win. I will pay more attention to any influence Peter Rathburn might have."

Drummond brought his hands together in one strong clap. "You see? Was that so difficult to admit?"

Nodding at the facility ahead, Max said, "We're here." He made no attempt to hide the relief in his voice.

Heritage Greens provided different levels of care for its residents. Everything from detached homes in which caregivers would visit once a day to apartment-style living which could provide round-the-clock care, if necessary. Though Joe Pardini lived on the third floor of one of these apartment buildings, the receptionist in the lobby assured Max that Mr. Pardini could easily live in one of the duplexes but chose to remain in the small apartment. Drummond snickered, but Max did not ask the ghost for further elaboration. For one thing, people mulled about the lobby and would find it strange to see Max talking to an empty space. For another thing, Max had enough of

Drummond's wit for the moment.

Drummond, however, had other ideas. On the elevator ride to the third floor, he said, "I don't think you were paying attention."

"I'm really not in the mood."

Drummond snapped his fingers. "This is an important interview. You need to start focusing."

Max could not hold back the incredulous look on his face. "You're the one who —"

"Do you really want to argue semantics right now? The fact is that you missed an important piece of information. Namely, that our pal Joey decided to stay in the apartment building rather than get his own place to live. A bigger place."

"So? He likes it here."

"Oh, he likes something all right."

Max paused as he thought over the implications. "You think he has the hots for one of the nurses?"

"Just as likely one of the other residents." As they walked down the hallway, Drummond flared his coat open and thrust his hands into his pants pockets. "Remember the things I've taught you. Pay attention to the little details. That's where the truth reveals itself."

Max knocked on the door for Room 317. Gazing up and down the hallway, he attempted to will himself into a higher level of observation. But the hallway struck him as nothing special — no more or less impressive than an average hotel corridor. He heard news reports on loud television sets echoing down the hall. He heard nurses asking questions of their patients and receiving louder responses. Now that Max thought of it, more like a hospital than a hotel.

Joe Pardini answered his door with a wide smile. "Come on in." He spoke louder, too, but Max thought the volume came from exuberance, not lack of hearing. Everything about the man was exuberant. He was short but made big gestures. His pudgy face overflowed with joy. He wore clean slacks, a nice shirt, and a bright, orange tie — Max wondered if he had dressed up simply for this visit.

"Thank you for agreeing to meet with me," Max said.

"I've been waiting decades for somebody to show an interest in this case." Patting his bald head like a bongo drum, Joe added, "Where are my manners? Please, have a seat."

Joe set two cups of coffee on a small table. Max sat and politely sipped from his cup. Not bad. Certainly better than he was expecting. Joe downed two large gulps and flashed another grin. "I almost forgot." Back on his feet, the man disappeared down a short hall.

As they waited, Drummond studied the room and Max followed suit. The apartment consisted mostly of a long, rectangular section with a kitchenette taking up the far end. The hall off to the right poked away only a few feet with doors for the bedroom, bathroom, and a small closet. From the items on the walls, the books on the shelves, and the odds and ends scattered throughout, Max surmised that Joe was a man of three specific passions. He liked to read old Westerns — Louis L'Amour, Zane Grey, and Max Brand. He liked sports — particularly the Carolina Panthers and the Demon Deacons. But most of all, he never stopped thinking about Vietnam. Pictures and flags were displayed on his walls. Two full shelves of books covered most every aspect of the subject. Several DVDs lay open on his coffee table — *Apocalypse Now, Platoon, Born on the Fourth of July*.

Drummond stopped in front of one photo. "This is definitely the right place to be."

Max walked over and found a faded picture of four soldiers standing in front of a latrine. The hot Vietnam sun burned down upon them, but they all wore innocent smiles. Max guessed the shortest of the four was Joe. There was no mistaking Wade Johnson — he looked identical to the photographs Max had seen in the newspapers.

"That was a great day," Joe said as he returned. "They said that digging a latrine would bring the best out in a bunch of screw ups, but we had such good laughs. Called ourselves the Crap Brothers." He sat at the table again and gulped more coffee. He had brought with him a manila envelope and pulled out several photographs.

As Drummond drifted over to check out the photos, he said, "This guy drinks coffee like he's trying to drown a camel."

Joe fluttered his hands at Max. "Sit, sit. I want you to see." He handed over two photographs. "I took both of those — probably should have been working for Stars and Stripes taking pictures of the war, but instead, they stick a rifle in my hands. Well, that's the way of it. One on the left is from camp. The one on the right, that one I took the day Wade came home. I think those two pictures tell the whole story."

Max examined the photographs closely. The first one showed Wade at his high school gymnasium. In the background, numerous other young men stood with their parents and loved ones as they prepared to board buses headed towards Boot Camp. Wade's bright eyes and charming smile lit up the photograph with youthful cockiness that suggested he knew everything would work out fine. In the second photo, Vietnam had taken its toll. Wade's straight-lined mouth and distant stare drained all life from the photo.

Tapping the darker image, Joe said, "He wasn't the same man when he came back. None of us were. We all had seen some horrible things, crap you wouldn't want your worst enemy to have to deal with, and we survived. Many of us weren't so lucky. I know how I sound, but that's the truth."

"I'm a bit confused," Max said, placing the photographs on the table. "How did you take this second photo? Weren't you still in Vietnam?"

Drummond soared back to the table. "Good question."

"I did my one tour and that was it. I came home. But Wade went back for a second go. He never should have done that. Even after a full tour, he still had stars in his eyes when it came to being a soldier. At least, that's how I saw it. When he came back, though, he didn't come back whole. I think that's what made him snap."

"I thought you were going to try to convince me that Wade was innocent."

"He is innocent. But that doesn't mean it was all easy. Holly had to fight hard to coax Wade's mind back from the war. And he snapped several times. Holly would call me in the middle of the night hysterical because Wade had grabbed his pistol and ran off into the woods. Stuff like that. But she always had the ability to bring him back to reality."

"You don't think he could have lost it one too many times? Turned his rage and his confusion upon the one he loved?"

Joe pointed at Max as if catching him in a trap. He pulled out a third photograph from his envelope. "This photo I took about a week before the murder."

Max saw Wade Johnson with his arm around Holly Claypool. Dressed in swimsuits, they stood in front of a wide lake. Though not as optimistic as the first photograph, this one brought back a sense of hope. Wade had a smile and his eyes gazed down at Holly with sincere love. If anything, Holly bore the distant stare, the troubled mouth.

Joe said, "I don't care what anybody thinks, that is not the picture of a man on the verge of killing the one he loves."

Drifting back to the picture on the wall, Drummond said, "You've been letting him control this interview. Time to shake it up. Ask him who these other two fellows are."

Max did as instructed, and Joe replied, "The guy on the far left was Mickey Carter. He was a real clown. In fact, it was his idea to call us the Crap Brothers and take this photo in front of our latrine. He could make us laugh — not an easy thing to do in the middle of a war." Joe paused and lowered his head. "About halfway through his tour, he was attached to a night patrol unit. Didn't make it back."

"I'm sorry," Max said.

Clearing his throat, Joe went on, "The other guy is Donnie Blackwell. Donnie didn't take it well what happened to Wade. Thought it just represented more of the horrible way we were being treated as vets. He disappeared. Well, I let him disappear. Guys like him, sometimes they drop off. Tune out. So I let him. Haven't spoken to him in maybe twenty years. Don't know where you could find him."

Joe's cell phone lit up and the grizzled voice of John Fogarty belted out his tune praising Susie Q. Turning off his cell phone alarm, he said, "You came at the right time. Do you like muffins?" With extra pep, Joe bounded across the room to check his appearance in the mirror. He flung on a baby blue coat and opened the front door.

Drummond slipped in beside Max. "I'll bet you anything we're about to meet the reason Joe didn't want to leave this crummy apartment."

They followed Joe as he ventured down the hall. At the end, he turned left and continued on. As they neared their destination, Max smelled the enticing aroma of baked goods.

Joe rapped a jaunty rhythm on the door of room 343. A charming woman answered. Her white hair sculpted close to her head, and her small features gave the impression of a person much younger than she was. Resting her head against the door, she reached out and took Joe's hand.

Smiling at Max, she said, "I see you brought company."

"I hope you don't mind," Joe said. "When I told this fellow about how good your muffins are, he just had to try them."

The woman blushed as she pulled Joe inside. "You are such a kidder." She waved Max in. "It's only blueberry today, nothing special. And I'm only an average baker. Especially in this small kitchen. But you're welcome to have a try if you'd like."

Drummond flew in first. "I'll bet she baked quite a muffin when she was younger."

Max's stomach rumbled at the delicious aroma as he looked around. When it came to decor, Max had learned that most elderly women fell into one of two camps. There were the collectors — those who attempted to hold onto their past by accumulating every memento, photograph, or knickknack that reminded them of days gone by. The other group were the grandmothers. They encompassed a wide-ranging spectrum but at the core, they dressed their homes to be warm and inviting. Sometimes the warmth could feel smothering or the invitation felt stiff but their heart always shined through. This woman definitely belonged to the latter group.

"Here, here," Joe said as he hurried towards Max with a large blueberry muffin in one hand. "You gotta give this a taste."

"Oh, leave the boy alone." The woman eagerly watched Max's expression.

To be polite and to quell his stomach, Max took a bite. He had to admit it was the best muffin he had ever eaten. Joe must have seen it on his face. The man laughed and gave Max a hearty thump on the back.

"I told you so. Stephie here is the best baker you've ever met."

Max nodded. "You could make a fortune with these."

Pouring batter into a clean muffin tin, Stephie said, "No. I make these for the residents. They're our little family and the joy is for us to share with each other."

"Yeah, but I'm not kidding. I can see people devouring these things all over the world."

"Not every success has to be a worldwide event."

Joe beamed as he wiped his mouth with a paper napkin. Promising to return once Max left, Joe led the way back to his apartment. Max had considered taking a muffin to go but decided that would be bad form. Drummond laughed at him. Back in the apartment, Joe poured another cup of coffee. "Thanks for indulging me. I hate to miss that woman's baking."

Drummond said, "I think he's after other kinds of muffins."

Rather than shoot Drummond any kind of expression, Max focused his energy on Joe. In order to maintain control of the interview, Max needed to direct these final questions — particularly making sure that Joe did not diverge off on a tangent.

He decided to go for shock value. "Did Wade ever mess around with the occult? Did he believe in witches or magic or anything like that?"

Joe cocked an eyebrow. "No. Never. What kind of question is that?"

"How about Holly? Did she have those kinds of interests?" Max could feel Drummond's approval. One clear way to control an interview that Drummond had taught him — if the subject tries to ask questions, only answer those that further your agenda. Otherwise, ask a new question.

Joe drained his coffee cup. "Not sure about Holly. Wade never mentioned anything like that about her. I find it kind of hard to believe. She was such a free spirit. You know who you should talk to is her brother, Floyd."

"You think Floyd Claypool killed his sister and Wade?"

Joe snorted a laugh. "No, no. He couldn't kill his sister. But his personality was always off a bit. Know what I mean?"

"Are you saying you think he's into the occult?"

"What's with the occult questions? No. He was always just a bit weird, that's all. I'm not saying he was into witchcraft or anything. Never once did I ever get any reason to think that, okay? But I always felt like he was hiding something. Even before the murder. He was overprotective of Holly, always keeping track of her whereabouts. That kind of thing. Oh, and he hated Wade. But afterwards, I remember meeting him at the funeral. He had this dazed look like a little kid lost at the mall. That's understandable, of course, but something always felt ... well, off. That's the only word I can give you. I don't know what I'm trying to say. I'm not doing a very good job of it. I guess I'm just saying that if you want more information on this, he is the guy I'd talk to."

Chapter 7

A QUICK SEARCH ON THE INTERNET produced only one Floyd Claypool living in the Triad — specifically, in the southern part of Winston-Salem. Max called Floyd and surprisingly, the man agreed to meet without any hesitation. However, he refused to meet at his home.

"It's Saturday," Floyd had said. "I fly my planes on Saturday. You can find me at Hobby Park from 11 to 2."

When Max arrived at the park, he found four men varying in age from mid-20s up to early-70s. All of them had remote control model airplanes. Several men hung out beneath a pagoda. They took turns soaring their buzzing aircraft in the sky and practicing takeoffs and landings on the park grass.

Max had no difficulty finding Floyd — he was the only seventy-year-old man there — and Floyd clearly had no trouble picking out Max — he was probably the only new face to come to the park in ages. Drummond drifted at Max's side, his eyes inspecting every detail.

As Floyd approached, Max saw a male version of Holly Claypool. Heavier, wrinkled, and bearing a grizzly, unshaven face. Unlike his sister, Floyd's nose had a sharp break in the middle. Still, the man shared the same breezy, hopeful air about him that his sister's photograph portrayed. Not entirely true, Max corrected himself — because he also noticed a darker undertone to Floyd's expression like a photograph taken at an angle that made the subject seem unsteady.

"You look like a reporter," Floyd said, his voice filled with threat.

Max put out his hand. "No, sir. Not a reporter. But I am investigating your sister's murder. I was hoping I could ask you a few questions."

"What are you? Cop?"

"Private investigator of sorts." Max's hand dangled in the air until he finally lowered it.

Floyd rocked on his heels. "Who's paying you to look into my sister's murder?"

"I'm not allowed to tell you that."

As a breeze passed between them, Floyd stared at Max, clearly trying to get a measure of the man. Drummond flew over to where Floyd's model plane had been parked. He checked it out for a quick second before hurrying back. "He's got a World War II Corsair there. Ask him about that."

Max motioned with his head toward the plane. "You a World War II buff? It's hard to tell from here, but I think that's a Corsair. Right?"

The corner of Floyd's mouth lifted. He turned around and walked toward his plane, a slight limp to his step. "Sure is. My father flew them in the war."

Max hustled to catch up. As Floyd fussed with various parts of the model as well as the remote control unit, he answered several questions regarding the hobby of flying and several more about his father's involvement in the war. Turned out the senior Claypool also flew one of the gliders that dropped the paratroopers ahead of D-Day. At length, Floyd set the remote control on the ground and sat next to his plane — not an easy feat at seventy.

"You're not going to tell me who hired you. Can you at least tell me what it is you want to know?"

"For starters," Max said, making sure not to sound too eager, "do you really think Wade Johnson did it?"

"Of course. The police investigated, and they had no doubts. Besides, why would the guy kill himself, if he hadn't been guilty?"

"Did you notice anything odd about his behavior leading up to that day?"

Floyd ripped grass from the ground and tossed it aside. "I tried not to pay too much attention to that bastard."

Drummond hovered closer. "Stay off of Wade. Focus on

the sister. That's your in."

Max nodded. "From what I can tell, you're absolutely right. Your sister was a devoted gal."

"She was. Always took good care of the people she loved. Loyal to a fault. The best."

Kneeling on the grass, he said, "Tell me more about her, please. I found lots about Wade, but newspaper articles rarely go into details about the victims. Don't they deserve to have their stories told?"

Floyd inhaled deeply as he brushed one knuckle under his eye. Max did not see evidence of a tear but the shiver in the man's voice suggested otherwise. "My sister and I had to look out for each other our whole life. Our parents died when I was fourteen — car accident. My old man survived D-Day, but a drunk on the road takes him out. Terrible. From that point on I tried to be the man of the house and take care of Holly. But you know what? She quickly took on a lot of the responsibilities, too. She ended up taking care of me as much as I took care of her. And things went fine for the next five years.

"Vietnam came, but they were never gonna send me. Not only was I Holly's sole guardian, but I have a bad knee from a time when I fell out of a treehouse as a kid. I'd never pass the Army physical."

"Was Wade her first boyfriend?"

"He was the first one she really got serious about. And he was the first one who stood up to me. Not an easy thing to do back then. Just because I didn't qualify for Vietnam didn't mean I wasn't a strong man. I took my responsibilities for her seriously, and any guy she wanted to date had come to through me first." Floyd chuckled. "Perhaps I was a little too protective."

"It was the late-60s. A lot of turmoil in the world at that time and a lot of behavior a parent, or in your case a guardian, would not approve of."

"The funny thing is that I'm not much older than her. Yet there I was acting like I was twenty years older. You have any kids?"

Max opened his mouth to answer but paused. With a surprised lilt, he said, "I guess I do."

"You guess?"

"My wife and I are in the process of becoming guardians ourselves — for two boys."

"Then you might know better than most how I felt."

"They're not at dating age yet, but I can still imagine."

One of the middle-aged men in the pagoda called over. "Hey, Floyd, you going up?"

Springing to his feet, Floyd picked up his large model and carried it over to the runway. Not the usual way of doing things — or so Max gathered from watching the others — but Floyd did not seem bothered. He started the engine, it's high-pitched buzz less impressive than its real-life counterpart, and in moments, Floyd had the aircraft floating through the air. Using his remote control unit, he dived and banked and attempted several acrobatic feats. All the while he gazed at the sky as if he could fly alongside his plane.

Max watched, letting his inner-child enjoy the marvel of a simple toy. The men at this park would probably pummel him if they knew he thought of these aircraft as toys. Strolling up to Floyd, he said, "I have just a few more questions."

Keeping his eyes on the plane, Floyd said, "You don't need to ask anything. It's not that complicated. Wade Johnson was no good from the start. Doesn't surprise me at all that he murdered my sister. That whole Johnson family was rotten to the core."

"What makes you say that?"

"Sometimes you can just tell. When I first met him, I knew what was on his mind — we're all guys. Besides, I was only a year older than him. Women were on my mind, too."

"Except his focus was Holly."

"I didn't like that one bit. I'm supposed to protect her, and I couldn't have him trying to make moves on her. Back then, getting pregnant out of wedlock was still taboo. Not as bad as years earlier, but bad enough. He was already signed up to go off to war, a fact that he liked to shove in my face whenever possible, so I knew he'd be pressuring Holly whenever he had the chance. No soldier wants to go off to die a virgin. And Holly had the kind of heart that would give her virginity to the man so that he might feel better about facing Death."

Floyd guided his Corsair around for one more turn and then brought it to a safe landing. The plane touched down without much of a bounce and taxied straight to Max's feet.

Max said, "You know, I met one of Wade's old army buddies — Joe Pardini. He had nothing but good to say about Wade. Painted quite a different picture than the one you're telling me."

"I'll bet." With the engine cut, Floyd checked over his plane. He had the care and attention of a mother bathing her baby. "I always thought Joe brought as much trouble as Wade. That boy liked to party it up. Heavy drinker, too. I could never prove it, but I have my suspicions about him."

"Suspicions?"

"He spent too much time defending Wade. Too much time trying to say it could never have happened, even though it did. Now, I'm not saying Joe was there or that he had any direct involvement with the murder, but at the very least, I would not be surprised to learn that he had something to do with planning. Probably had the whole thing laid out including how they'd get away with it. He just didn't expect Wade's guilt to take over. Didn't think Wade would kill himself." Biting his bottom lip, Floyd pushed the antenna on his remote control down. "I guess that's all for today. The wind is picking up a bit and I'm tired. You got any more questions?"

"I guess not. Do you mind if I call you should something else come up?"

Floyd shrugged. "Don't know what else I could help you with. If you really want more of the story, you should meet with the other one — Donnie something. Donnie Blackwell. He's the other member of that squad who's still alive."

"I don't recall seeing his name connected with the murder. How's he involved?"

"He's not. As far as I know. But he knew Wade better than

most. Joe likes to act like they were close buddies, but from everything I heard, it was Donnie and Wade to the end. If you're trying to figure out Wade Johnson, your best bet is Donnie Blackwell."

"Thanks for the suggestion."

"Sure. Don't ask me where he is. I never really met the man. Just heard about him. You've got to check with the VFW. They should know where to find him."

Without another word, Floyd picked up his plane and ambled away. Max could feel the air chill at his side as Drummond floated in.

"That was strange," Drummond said.

"His eagerness to talk? Or the fact that he really never pressed us for why I was looking into his sister's murder?"

"Exactly."

Chapter 8

AS THE SUN LOWERED to close out the day, overcast clouds rolled in. Fitting, Max thought as he drove toward the Mill Cemetery. If a thick fog crawled across the way, they would have the perfect setting for a graveyard visit. At least, Max had quiet for the moment — Drummond had gone off to the Other in search of Donnie Blackwell. According to the VFW, Donnie had died eleven years ago. They were cagey about how he had died, though. Hiding behind the excuse that Max was not family, they refused to divulge any more information. It was a silly argument — Max could find out the answers with a few minutes on the internet.

"This is a lot easier when we can simply chat with the victim's ghost," Max said to the empty car.

The idea bothered him more than he dared admit. Dealing with other-worldly cases all the time meant that they had to rely on Drummond and Sandra for the answers. Max was supposed to be the leader of the group, yet he had the least to offer. In truth, he was the least qualified.

He could hear Sandra's rebuttal in his head, pointing out that his research skills surpassed everybody else and that without those skills, they would never have found the right places to go looking for the answers that she and Drummond could find. It sounded nice. Believing it was another matter entirely.

This wasn't the first time he had entertained such dark thoughts of late, and he wondered if Mother Hope's curse upon him had influenced him in this way, too. The fact that the curse had not been designed to mess with his state of mind did not appease him — logic would have no place in this internal debate. Except the reasonable side of Max pointed out that perhaps he merely felt more pressure to prove his worth as those around him appeared to have finally settled into their roles within this ad hoc family.

Drummond appeared in the passenger seat and saved Max from spiraling into even darker thoughts. "Well, I've got good news and bad news."

"Isn't it always that way with you?"

"I don't make it, I just deliver it."

"Fine, fine. Did you find Donnie Blackwell?"

Drummond took off his hat, ran his fingers through his hair, and placed the hat back on. "Donnie is definitely not in the Other. That's the bad news. The good news is that every single one of my contacts in the Other told me the same thing — they never heard of a Donnie Blackwell and that they never saw him, either."

"That's good news?"

"You're not following. Every single one of them told me that. Every. Single. One. They're lying."

"So Donnie is in the Other?"

"No, that much they were telling the truth about. But they all made an effort to convince me that they had no knowledge of him or anything about where he might be."

"What does that mean then?"

Tapping his chin, Drummond said, "The way I read it is this — if we're lucky, we'll find Donnie hanging out by his grave. If not, then at least we know we're going down the right path."

"Because somebody has managed to scare your ghost contacts enough to stay quiet."

With a clap of his hands, Drummond smiled. "Exactly. You're really starting to get smart about this stuff — some of it, anyway."

Max parked in a gravel lot and the two walked into the cemetery. Spread out over two rolling hills with a church at the far end, the cemetery looked calm, peaceful, and troubling. That last one, Max acknowledged, probably only applied towards him and Drummond. More so for Drummond — Max had the benefit of not being able to see all the ghosts surrounding them. But watching Drummond nod, smile, wink, and even tip his hat as they walked up the gravel path, Max knew a small town of ghosts mulled about their endless, dreary day.

"Is it worth it to ask any of these ghosts?" Max asked.

Keeping his smile locked in place, Drummond said, "I wouldn't dare. Ghosts like these — ones stuck at the graveside — not the kind you want to be talking with. Some of them are over a hundred years old and still can't move on. These are ghosts that have real problems."

Checking his phone, Max swiped across a map of the grave plots he had downloaded earlier. "Just ahead," he said, leading the way to the grave of Donnie Blackwell. "Is he there?"

"Not unless he likes to wear dresses from the 1800s."

They proceeded onward until they reached a small headstone that read:

Donnie Blackwell
1951–1987
May peace be his eternal blessing

Gazing across the field of headstones, Max said, "I'm not trying to be funny, but it looks like we're at a dead end."

Drummond stared at the grave. "Except there's that." He gestured with his chin.

"There's what?"

Pointing at the headstone, Drummond said, "That. Seems pretty obvious what happened to Donnie."

Max looked over the headstone once more. "I'm missing something. What is it you think happened to Donnie?"

Drummond frowned as he moved closer to the headstone. He waved his hand in a circular motion around the center of the stone. "Do you not see the giant pentagram here?"

"I don't see anything except a standard headstone."

He tipped his hat back and whistled. "That's not good."

Max's stomach churned. "What exactly does that mean?"

"Don't know. But any kind of curse that only a ghost could

see — well, we're headed down a dangerous road."

"Seems about par for us."

Max brought up the camera on his phone and lined up the picture. He didn't think a ghostly curse would appear in the photograph, but it couldn't hurt to try. Perhaps Sandra would have better luck seeing something.

As he lined up a second angle, a large chunk of the headstone splintered off into the air. A moment later, Max heard the gunshot.

Chapter 9

MAX FLATTENED TO THE GROUND. He buried his face in the grass as another shot chipped off more of the gravestone. He only heard his shivering breath and the hammering of his heart. His mouth ran dry.

Drummond said, "Keep low and find good cover. I'll go stop this joker."

Getting shot at didn't seem like much of a joke, but as Drummond started across the cemetery, Max wriggled on his belly, using his elbows to propel forward. Another crack of gunshot echoed in the air. Max did not see where the bullet struck — *as long as it's not in me, I'm fine.*

He had to move faster. Even behind the gravestones, he did not feel safe. For one thing, he had no clue where the shots came from. If the shooter had any brains, he would shift positions after every few shots. The safety of the gravestones would not last once the shooter changed to a position where he could nail Max in the back.

Max lifted his head. Spitting grass from his mouth, he scanned the hillside. About thirty yards away, at the bottom of a small incline, a workshed stood — its single door ajar. Hell of a run, but if he made it, he'd be better off than sitting out here in the open.

Like a lizard, he belly-crawled to the end of the row of graves. He paused and listened. No shots rang out.

He wanted to call out to Drummond. Perhaps the old ghost had found the shooter and thrust his pale hand into the bastard's head. The resulting freeze would incapacitate the man. But if Drummond had succeeded, then why hadn't he called out to Max? Why didn't he tell Max to run?

The shooter was on the move. That was why things were

quiet. *And I have to move, too.*

Thirty yards. A long distance but not insurmountable. In his high school days, he had run a fifty yard dash regularly. He could do thirty with his eyes closed. Of course back then he was young, in good shape, and nobody had been shooting at him.

Max tucked his feet underneath and kept hunched over. Trying to remain as small a target as possible, he dug the toes of his shoes into the ground and readied to push off. The salt of his sweat trickled into his mouth. He tried to control his breathing but his lungs would not cooperate.

He heard a bang, and as if reacting to a starter pistol, he bolted into a full-on sprint. The first ten yards ripped by. Pumping his arms as fast as his legs, he cut across the field like a cheetah.

Halfway there, his mind registered the sound he had heard. Not a gunshot — rather, a car backfiring. That's when he heard the difference. A real bullet slammed into the ground less than a foot ahead of him. Pouring all the energy he had left into his legs, Max pushed harder.

The workshed came closer and closer. Only a few more yards. He thought he heard another shot, but he saw no evidence. An old soldier's saying sprang into his head — *you don't hear the bullet that kills you.* He hoped to keep hearing any gunshots as much as he hoped the gunshots would stop altogether.

The shed came up fast. Max's left foot caught the lip of the concrete base. Pain electrified his big toe. He stumbled forward into the shed and crashed against a barrel filled with shovels, rakes, and a pickax. Gasping for air, he stared at the doorway, wondering if his killer would appear. Spit fluttered off his lips. His eyes peered, not blinking. He knew he should move out of view of the doorway but he remained immobile — he'd given all he had to get that far.

Once more, he only heard his heart beating. Once more, he wondered if Drummond had rescued him. Once more, he waited.

"It's all clear," Drummond said, the frustration in his voice unmistakable. "He's gone. I missed him."

Drummond appeared in the doorway with one hand in his pocket and his head cocked to the side. He turned his gaze back to the tree line. "I looked for the flashes of light when he shot, but I never saw any. I had to go by sound, and by the time I reached wherever I thought the sound came from, he'd already moved on. If he was even in that spot to begin with. I must've gotten close the last time because he's definitely taken off."

Max got to his feet and forced himself to calm his breathing. "How do you know? He could be out there right now, waiting for me to put my head out."

"Not likely. He shot a lot of bullets. That made a lot of noise. He's got to know somebody will take notice. Even out here."

Despite Drummond's assurances, Max decided to run back to his car as fast as he could muster. Though his legs fought the idea and his stubbed toe complained the entire way, he still managed a speedy jog. Slamming the car door shut, he thrust the key into the ignition, and raced off.

"Slow down," Drummond said from the passenger seat. "You don't want to die on the road right after you managed to not die from a bullet."

Max eased back on the accelerator — but only a little. Though his hands still shook, he said, "This case is getting worse and worse. If I get shot at one more time, I swear—"

His cell phone rang and he jolted as if he had touched a live wire. He glanced at the phone — Sandra. Trying to sound as calm as possible, he answered. He need not have bothered — Sandra was too excited to notice his frazzled state.

"I've got it," she said. "I know what we're dealing with."

Chapter 10

MAX SAT BEHIND HIS OFFICE DESK and downed his third shot of whiskey. As its warmth spread through his body, he rested his head back and closed his eyes. "You'd think I'd be comfortable with people trying to kill me, but it doesn't get any easier."

Floating in the middle of the room, Drummond lay flat on his back with his legs crossed and his hands behind his head. "Be thankful it doesn't get easier. If that ever starts happening, it's time to get out of this business. Otherwise, you'll end up dead."

Max let silence fall upon them like an evening snow. He thought of nothing more than his jangled nerves. Each slow breath, he slipped closer toward sleep.

But the clamber of two energetic teens filled the hall as they raced toward the office door. The click of Sandra's heels followed behind.

The boys burst in like fraternity brothers returning from watching their team win. Big smiles and loud voices erupted as they raced across the room for Max. Sandra entered, also smiling broadly, but Max caught her exhaustion as well. This guardian gig would require more of them than they had realized.

"Max, Max, Max," J said, jumping around as if he needed to go to the bathroom.

"What? What? What?" Max said.

J laughed, and that wonderful sound reminded Max why they had wanted this in the first place. "You wouldn't believe the place we went to today. Sandra told us it was a store for witches, but it's really mostly old, dusty stuff. It was still really cool, though. They had all these weird smelling sticks, a zillion candles of every color you could think of, tons of books with the stupidest names — things I couldn't even pronounce — and everywhere you looked there was a stuffed animal staring back at you. I'm not kidding. In the corners of the room, on top of bookshelves, and there was even a little stuffed dog sitting at the door to the bathroom. It was crazy."

PB acted every bit as thrilled as J. "He's telling the truth. And the lady who ran the store was a real nutjob. She had this long nose and one eye was bigger than the other and she wore these really big earrings. She was dressed in all black, and spoke in this creaking kind of voice. Like a cartoon witch. And she tried to convince us that witches were real. I mean she really believed it and expected that we believed it, too."

As the boys rattled on their list of all the bizarre things they found in the cluttered store, Sandra walked behind Max and kissed the top of his head. He patted her hand as she continued to move around the desk. Without a word she lifted the whiskey flask and returned it to the hollowed out book on the shelf.

"This lady," J continued, "talked on and on about ghosts. I mean, ghosts. You believe that?"

"Of course he does," PB said. "We don't call him Ghostman for nothing."

"But these were different. What did she call them?"

"Torn ghosts." PB barely managed to say the words without giggling as if this were the funniest phrase they had ever heard. "Now I know that's code for something else, but Sandra refuses to tell us what."

Max pushed his chair back. "Don't look to me. That's my wife you're talking about. I'm not crossing her."

PB pointed right at Max. "Then you admit it — it is a code for something else. If it weren't, you'd have nothing to worry about crossing her over."

"I'm not admitting anything. If those ladies say there are ghosts, then I'm going to believe there are ghosts."

PB exchanged a curious look with J. Before they could formulate another angle to question Max, the office door opened and in walked Mrs. Porter. Both boys scrambled towards her and shouted, "Grandma!"

Mrs. Porter knelt down and hugged them. She fussed with their shirts and hair, and though they made efforts to escape her touch, Max could see how much they enjoyed having adults around who cared about them.

"Well," Mrs. Porter said as if she were speaking with much younger children, "it looks like you boys are going to be with me tonight."

J said, "Can we stay a little longer? Please?"

"Yeah, we just got here," PB chimed in. "We haven't finished telling Max all about what we saw today."

Mrs. Porter crossed her arms. "You'll have to settle for telling me. We need to let Max and Sandra get their work done. Tomorrow is for homework and then school on Monday. You get to see them on Monday night and you can tell Max all about whatever it is you want to tell him then."

Though their enthusiasm diminished, they did not put up a fight when it came to leaving the office. Mrs. Porter glanced back at Max and winked. She waved goodbye and mouthed the words *I'll call you tomorrow. Love you.*

When the boys left, Max's heart dropped as if watching the boys swept out to sea. He thumbed the edge of his desk as he thought. "We shouldn't let her keep doing our job."

Sandra slumped into her chair. "Speak for yourself. I've been with them all day."

"That's not what I mean. They're already calling her Grandma, but us — we're just Max and Sandra."

"I know." Sandra rubbed her eyes like a doctor on her thirtieth hour of a forty-eight hour shift. "It'll take time. And it takes us being there more."

"That's what I'm saying. We can't let my mom keep leaving with them."

"Honey, it's kind of hard to have the business conversations we need to have with them in the room."

Drummond waved from the ceiling. "She's talking about me."

Max gave a sarcastic thumbs-up. To Sandra, he said, "All I'm saying is that if we're serious about doing this, about making all of us a family, then we've got to work harder at it." He sat up and put out his hand to stop Sandra from reacting. "I'm not saying you weren't there with them today. I'm saying that maybe it's time we tell them the truth."

"Are you nuts?" Drummond flew down to stand in the middle of the floor.

Sandra weighed the idea. "It's going to be difficult to convince them without scaring the hell out of them."

"Absolutely," Max said. "And I don't know how to convince them when they can't see any of it. At least, I can see Drummond. I don't know. Maybe it's a stupid idea."

Drummond said, "I can agree with that. Listen, your heart's in the right place, but rarely have I seen things go well when trying to tell people about this world if they're not ready to believe it. They have to come to it on their own, discover the truth themselves. And if they don't have the ability to see even one ghost or experience one spell, then no amount of evidence will ever change their mind."

As if reaching out to Max with her eyes, Sandra said, "He might be right."

"He's definitely right," Drummond said. "I've been going through this a lot longer than you two. Trust me — if those boys are ever going to believe you guys, they'll figure it out on their own, and they'll let you know when they're ready to believe."

Max fidgeted with the edge of the table some more. "I don't know if I can agree with that, but I think it's something that we need to think about."

Drummond pushed his hat back. "Great. Now that we've settled that, how about we hear what Sandra found out?"

Both men focused their attention on her. Her face brightened, and she rummaged through her purse to pull out her notebook.

"The first thing you need to understand," she said, taking on a bit of the tone and attitude Max often used when sharing his research, "is that the idea of a torn ghost is more myth than fact. There are stories that go back centuries — most told from one witch to another as a caution when learning about curses. That's not to say that what we're dealing with isn't a torn ghost — in fact, I firmly believe that it is — but we need to be aware that these things are so rare, the information available on them is dubious at best."

Max said, "Dubious or not, it's the best we've got."

"That's right, doll," Drummond said with a wink. "We're all ears for you."

As Sandra referred to her notes once more, Max glimpsed her tolerant grin. No matter how hard they tried, Drummond would always be a man of his time. Specifically, the 1940s. He tried to update the way he spoke with women, but there were limits to how far he would ever be able to go. Even more than as a man, as a ghost, his mindset had been firmly put in place.

Stepping into the center of the room, Sandra cleared her throat. Drummond drifted backwards toward the wall.

Sandra said, "At its core, a torn ghost is one that was damaged at the moment the person died. Whatever part of us transfers from our body into whatever Drummond is—"

"I'm still all me."

"Then, whatever form you are — something goes wrong during that process, and the ghost becomes stuck in her final moments. She can't move on, she can't go to the Other, and she can't be a normal ghost. It's as if she were stuck on another plane of existence, one that makes it near-impossible for us to communicate with her. Even ghosts have difficulty seeing the torn ghosts."

"We certainly know that's true. I still haven't been able to contact her."

Focusing on Sandra's report helped clear Max's mind. His nerves drained away like water soaking into the ground. "When you say she's *stuck in her final moments* — does that mean Holly Claypool is reliving her death? Over and over like on repeat?"

Sandra's lips rolled in as she gave one shake of her head. "Nobody knows for sure. That's what a lot of witch lore suggests, but I also found a few books that outlined a far grimmer situation for her."

Drummond said, "This is like that ghost we dealt with in Alamance — the one that had shredded itself."

"That ghost had ripped itself to pieces trying to break free of a curse that tethered it to the battlefield it had died upon. This is different. There is no tether. There doesn't need to be one. She is stuck. And if she's not on a continuous loop of her final moments, it's possible that she has been stretched out between our world, the Other, and whatever happens when we move on. It could be that she has been stretched so thin, her ghostly form and even her mind are like rice paper. If that idea is true, then that's why we can't see her and it's difficult for ghosts to make contact with her — because she's not entirely there. But there are several other ideas I read about in these books. The only one that seems plausible, unless you want to start believing in reptile people that crawl out of the ground and attempt to possess your spirit, is one of emptiness. The concept here is that upon dying, instead of turning into a ghost or moving on, her spirit ended up making a wrong turn — she became nothing, empty, lost in a vast vacuum of nothingness. For eternity."

"If that last one were true," Max said, "then how is it that she could make contact with you or Irene Beck or anybody?"

"That's exactly how I saw it, but I wanted to give you the option in case you picked up on something I missed."

"This is all great stuff. But the big question is — did you find a way to help her? Or even just talk with her?"

"As far as the texts are concerned or even the people I spoke with, these things are practically fairytales. Nobody alive claims to actually have seen a torn ghost, and the books speak of them as if they were magic — and I don't mean the kind of magic which is actually performed. I mean like kid magic, like non-existent nonsense. That's why I began this by saying that it's more myth than anything else."

"Except this myth is actually hanging out in a Winston-Salem firehouse."

"Yeah, except that."

Drummond said, "At least now we know some of what we're dealing with. Max, you should fill in Sandra on everything we've learned today. Go straight up to the point you got shot at."

Sandra whirled at Max. "You were shot at?"

Eyeballing Drummond like a disappointed parent, Max said, "Yeah, but I'm okay." Before Sandra could release a tidal wave of questions, Max explained their route of investigation throughout the day. When he finished, they sat in silence and digested everything.

Sandra rocked back in her chair. "It seems to me that we've got a lot of pieces which should definitely connect. Anybody know how?"

"Not yet," Max said. "We know several of the players, and we may know the end results beyond Holly getting murdered. But we don't know any of the how or why, and we can't really be sure about Holly being a torn ghost. As you pointed out, torn ghosts could be more myth than anything else."

Drummond floated in a thoughtful circle above them. "It is a lot to hang the entire case on — something we can't see or hear or even verify."

"And of the living ones, who do we believe?" Sandra said. "Floyd or Joe?"

"They might both be telling the truth — from their points of view."

Max drove his heel into the edge of his table. "What I'm hearing is that we have gathered a ton of information which has led us nowhere."

"Not true. You got shot at today. That means we're closer to some sort of answer — certainly closer than somebody is happy about."

Sandra's gaze dropped to the circular rug on the floor. Underneath it, carved into the wood, was a casting circle. Max snapped his fingers to get her attention. "I thought you said there was no spell to contact these torn ghosts. What are you thinking?"

She leaned forward and rested her chin on her fist. "I was thinking that all the texts I read said no one spell could succeed. But what if you have a whole coven of witches working in tandem? We've seen that happen before for other kinds of spells."

"You are not seriously suggesting we go contact the more powerful witches that we know."

"Not yet. But we should keep that option open."

"Are you both nuts?" Drummond said, pointing at them like an angry conductor. "Haven't you had enough bad experiences to understand that messing around with witches and covens is only going to get you hurt? If this torn ghost thing is true, then there has to be a way to help her that doesn't involve messing with covens. There's a natural balance in the universe — good balances with evil. If you ask me, whatever created a torn ghost is evil which means that some form of good is what's going to fix this. Not messing with a coven."

Sandra raised her voice. "It was just a thought."

"Not a good one."

Like a coach calling for timeout, Max put up his hands to form a T. "I'm not interested in getting shot at again, so we need to come up with a way forward. Sandra, perhaps you can hit the books some more, see if there's anything else that can provide us with a direction. Drummond, why don't you go back into the Other. See if you can get any leads on Wade Johnson — I'm guessing he is also a torn ghost, but maybe one of your contacts knows something. We've got to find a way to talk with Holly, and we've got to do it before we all get shot at."

Sandra locked eyes with Max. He tried to look strong, but she must have seen the fear trembling throughout him. Her chin quivered as her eyes glistened.

She rushed over and held him with all the strength of a wife determined to protect her husband. He was glad — sometimes all he really needed came from being in her arms. She kissed him lightly. "I can go through all the books I have again, but I don't think we're going to find anything. I don't mean to be negative, I'm only trying to be efficient. You said it yourself, somebody's trying to kill you. They might come after me as well. I don't want to waste time searching books that I know don't have the answers." She glanced over at Drummond. "Same goes for you. Is there really anything you can find in the Other that you didn't find when you were there earlier?"

Drummond's jaw jutted out as he crossed his arms. Muttering to himself, he drifted aimlessly backwards. Wiping their eyes, Max and Sandra stood as they watched their partner. At length, Drummond leveled a cold stare at Max. "You really think the shooter's going to come back?"

"Don't you?"

With regret, Drummond nodded. "In that case, I have a suggestion."

Sandra stepped around the desk, moving closer to Drummond while reaching back for Max's hand. "What do you know?"

"You ever hear of witch's water?"

Sandra shook her head and looked back at Max. He shrugged.

"You've certainly heard of holy water," Drummond said. "That's just regular water that's been given a blessing by a holy man. The holy man comes along says a few words and suddenly you have holy water. It's a magic spell. People don't like to think of it that way, but it's the truth."

Max said, "I take it witch's water is water that's been spelled by a witch."

"Yeah. But it's a hard spell. And it's harder to find a witch willing to do it."

"Why? What's wrong with the stuff?"

"Witch's water is powerful. You pour it in a circle, and it will create an instant conduit with the ghosts in a room. Summon them up, get them talking. You don't even have to have magical ability. Anybody can use this water. You don't even have to say a spell or know special ingredients. No hand motions or meditation. Nothing. You just pour the circle and it does the rest."

Sandra said, "What's the catch?"

"It's extremely volatile, for one. And it doesn't always connect the way you want it to. I've only ever used it once, and that time, it took an angry ghost with limited contact to the world and set her loose with a rage that killed people. Also, sometimes witch's water explodes."

With a short laugh, Max said, "So, if I got this, witch's water can make contact with an otherwise inaccessible ghost but it may explode on us or turn the ghost into something akin to a poltergeist. That about right? Or will it also melt my face off? Because, you know, I like my face, and I'm pretty sure Sandra likes it, too."

"Do I look like I'm joking around?" Not only did Drummond look unamused, Max could not think of a time he had seen such a horrible seriousness on the ghost's face.

Sandra said, "You must think this stuff could really work. Otherwise, given the risks, you wouldn't suggest it."

"It's dangerous. It works by bringing a ghost into the corporeal world. You're not talking to it through some kind of magic phone line — it really comes here. You both know how painful it is for me to touch the physical world, can you imagine what would happen if we yanked a torn ghost into this place? It may not be worth it. But I can't think of any other possible way to get in contact with her."

"Sitting around waiting for Max and I to get shot at is not an option. I say we get this special water."

"That's why I mentioned it. I don't want to see either of you take a bullet."

"Fine," Max said. "How do we get the stuff?"

Drummond faced the window and closed his eyes. "Yeah, you're not going to like that answer."

"I don't like any of this. Out with it."

"Witch's water is difficult to acquire because most witches won't make it. Not only is it dangerous and in some cases deadly, but because it allows every common Joe a chance to cast magic, it makes magic seem less special. That doesn't sit well with the coven crowd."

Max slid back into his chair. He saw where this was going, and it made him want to throw up. Sandra must have figured it out as well because she said, "We'll need to make a deal with a witch, won't we?"

"A powerful witch," Drummond said.

"You're talking about Mother Hope."

"She's the only one I can think of that you might convince to help you. The Magi are supposed to be set up to control witches and protect regular people. Perhaps she'll help out when she realizes we're dealing with a torn ghost. Especially one that's hurting the fire department. Point out to her that this ghost is costing real lives when the firefighters can't do their job properly. That might work. She's a power-mad lunatic, but she got into it all for noble reasons. That part of her might still be inside. Somewhere."

"There's also the Mobley coven."

"That's even worse that dealing with the Magi and Mother Hope."

Max's stomach twisted more, and he placed his head on the cool desk blotter. "We're not going to Mother Hope and we're not going to the Mobleys either. In fact, we're not dealing with any witches at all. We have another way."

Lifting his head, he grinned. Sandra placed her hand on her hip, ready to argue, when her face brightened. "You're talking about Leon Moore."

"You said it yourself — we've got to make use of the man. Otherwise, what was the point of going through all we did with him?"

Drummond rubbed his hands together. "Then let's talk to old Leon."

Chapter 11

THE FOLLOWING MORNING, Max sat at the breakfast table with Sandra and Drummond discussing how they would approach their meeting with Leon Moore. Before heading home the previous night, Max had phoned Leon and told him to be available at eleven in the morning. Leon hesitated, uttered a few guttural sounds, and then agreed.

"That's good," Drummond had said as he slipped into his bookcase for the night. "He didn't argue with you, didn't even negotiate the time — he knows what having that curse means. We might actually have a chance of pulling this off."

After a few hours of fitful sleep, Max wondered if Drummond had been too optimistic. Nobody in their right mind would attempt to steal witch's water from one as powerful as Mother Hope. But then, Drummond kept pointing out that Leon had this curse on him — and curses often put people out of their right mind.

Max stabbed at his eggs while Sandra spread jam on her toast. Drummond watched and made a slim attempt to hide his envy — the poor ghost had not eaten in almost eighty years.

"We're agreed then?" Max said. "As long as Leon does not have a ward against ghosts, the three of us sit down and play a bit of good cop–bad cop–ghost cop."

Drummond said, "That'll work fine. Since you're the one who put the curse on him, you play bad cop. Sandra acts all warm and smiles, and if he still resists, then I'll pass a hand or two through them and he'll get the message."

Sandra washed down her toast with a cup of coffee. "We've dealt with Leon many times. We know what his strengths are and his weaknesses. This time, we have the advantage. That's why we cursed him. For this kind of advantage. Let's calm down and rely on what we have set up. Trust ourselves."

"Once again, your wife shows us how smart she is. You really ought to let her run things."

Max bristled, but when he spoke, he kept his voice even and calm. "I agree that we're going into this with an advantage. It's important that we not get complacent, though. If I learned anything from this old ghost here, it's that the moment you think you have everything going your way, that's when it all falls apart."

Sandra's cellphone rang as Drummond leaned on his elbows toward Max. "Looks like you have been listening to me."

Sandra left the table and walked into the living room. Though she greeted the caller with a cheery voice, Max noticed her concerned brow. He tried to keep an ear on her end of the conversation, but Drummond rattled on about his success with their student-mentor relationship and how Max shouldn't get cocky because there still existed a mountain of knowledge to climb. When she returned to the kitchen, she grabbed her plate and began cleaning up by the sink. Max simply stared at her. After all these years together, he knew that she would speak in a few seconds — though the longer it took her, the worse he thought the news would be.

At length, she said, "That was our client, Peter Rathburn."

Drummond whipped his head toward her. "That doesn't sound good."

"Did something happen?" Max asked. "Another incident?"

Though they had a perfectly good dishwasher, Sandra scrubbed the plates by hand. Keeping her focus on the task, she said, "No, nothing like that. Everything is fine." For everything being fine, she sure seemed to be scrubbing quite hard. "Peter simply wants me to meet him to give a full update on our progress — over lunch."

"Right," Drummond said, drawing the word out.

Sandra shoved a dirty pan into the sink. Thrusting a soapy washcloth in Drummond's direction, she said, "Don't you start acting like that. The man is our client, and he's paying our bills. If he wants to meet us to discuss the case, then that's what'll happen."

"Except he doesn't want to meet us, does he?"

Her eyes darted to Max before rushing back to the sink. "He asked for me specifically. That's because he's comfortable with me. He knows me. Besides, you two have to go visit Leon."

Max picked up his plate and walked over to her side. With a more personal tone, he said, "Are you saying this lunch is set for the same time we're talking with Leon?"

"He said he wanted to beat the Sunday church crowd. You know what it's like if you wait till noon — you can't find a table anywhere."

"But we need you. Good cop-bad cop doesn't work with just a bad cop."

Forcing a smile, Sandra looked at her husband. "You'll have to come up with a different plan. I know you can do it. We don't have a choice in the matter, so let's not argue about it and just make it work." Pushing forward, she gave Max a tight hug and a strong kiss. As she backed away, she said, "I better go get ready."

She escaped upstairs, leaving Max standing in the kitchen with a dumbfounded look and only a sarcastic ghost by his side.

Though they had forty-five minutes until the meeting and the drive to Wake Forest University only took ten, Max insisted on leaving. Drummond could have stayed behind and appeared when needed, but he tagged along anyway. Max said nothing during the short car ride, and Drummond did the same.

He parked at his favorite spot near the biology building and sat without a sound. Sunday morning on any college campus felt empty, and this was no different. A single jogger went by, huffing along the curved road, and headed uphill. This case felt much the same, and Max wondered how steep the hill ahead might become. At least the jogger knew what path to follow. Max didn't even have that much.

After about four minutes of quiet, from the corner of his eye, he caught Drummond staring back at him. The ghost would face away and look out the window, but only moments later, his focus returned. Max said nothing.

Let him stare.

He knew better than to think Drummond would stay quiet for long. As if suffering from stomach cramps, the ghost brought his hat down to his belly. He made a slight motion with his head before he spoke. "I'm only going to say this because I don't want to see things get any worse between you two. Trust me here — you cannot let this Rathburn fellow continue to worm his way into your wife's life."

"For the last time, I trust Sandra. That's all that matters."

"If you believe that, then why are you sitting in this parking lot fuming mad?"

"I'm having a bad morning. Do me a favor and shut up."

"You'll have a lot more bad mornings if you don't pay attention to what I'm saying."

Max slammed his hand on the steering wheel. "In twenty minutes, I have to go convince a man to defy one of the most powerful witches around. I don't have time to worry about Peter's nefarious plotting to undermine my marriage. If he seriously thinks that Sandra is so easily manipulated, then he's going to be very disappointed. And where's all this coming from? You've known Sandra for years now. What makes you think that some guy she knew for a year or two, decades ago, could succeed in breaking up our marriage?"

"It's not like that. You aren't listening."

Max rubbed the side of his face and sighed. "Do me a favor and go to the Other. See if you can find somebody to help us. Or go somewhere else. Just leave me in peace so I can prepare to deal with Leon."

Drummond set his hat back on his head and adjusted his coat. "Sheesh. Try to help out a guy and this is the thanks I get. Good luck on your own."

Max instantly regretted his words, but when he turned to apologize, Drummond had already disappeared. Getting out of the car, a single raindrop hit Max's cheek. The gray sky promised a chilly, wet day. He locked the car and headed toward the Z Smith Reynolds Library.

He should have brought a heavier jacket. Then again, even

with the rain, chances were high that by the end of the day, he would be uncomfortably warm. Max had learned that the only consistency in Southern weather was its inconsistency.

The grayness of the day turned Wake's lovely campus into a stark, damp maze of walkways and buildings. The sounds deadened, closing around him, but the quiet only heightened the fact that he walked without Sandra, without Drummond, without a plan.

Sandra. He could picture her having lunch with Peter, picture the way she smiled politely but kept a cool distance. She would give the report on their progress, keep everything formal. Sure, they might reminisce a little, but Peter would be a fool to think he could steal her heart based on some ancient high school romance.

Drummond was wrong. Simple as that. For all his knowledge, that ghost still thought in an outdated way.

Walking across an open courtyard surrounded by several old brick buildings, Max spied a middle-aged woman holding the hand of a young boy. As she hurried toward one of the buildings, the boy tried to yank free. Max could not hear what they said, but the muted tones and the expressions on their faces told him enough — the woman had an urgent thing to do in the building and brought her son with her because she had to. Sounded like her husband had left the marriage only recently. She promised and cajoled and even threatened the boy, but he still dragged his feet and pouted, never once taking notice of his mother's harried expression.

Max paused. Maybe Drummond had been right — just not in the way he thought. Maybe the real issue was the Sandwich Boys. Max and Sandra drew closer to becoming guardians every day. The boys had given their faith, their trust — perhaps Sandra was having second thoughts. The day before, she had looked exhausted after spending all that time with the two boys, and though she talked about spending more with them, it seemed there always was a case to be solved standing in the way.

They had never fought hard to have kids of their own. They

were happy just the two of them. What if this was all too much?

No. He was being paranoid. The woman he loved had taught him to embrace these boys and their future. She was too strong to be cowed by fears like that.

"Which probably means the fears are mine," he muttered.

Checking his phone for the time, he picked up his pace. He entered the library from the side, and walked to the open study area he knew so well. Seeing the beautiful manner in which the two separate buildings had been connected to form a unique open structure never stopped filling Max with awe. He picked out a large rectangular table far enough removed from the handful of students using the Sunday morning quiet to get some work done.

Before he could settle in, Leon's deep grumble said, "I'm here. What the hell do you want?"

Chapter 12

WHEN MAX HAD FIRST MET LEON MOORE, the black man stood crooked, had a bulldog's wrinkles, and a sly attitude. Once Leon involved himself with the Magi, the deal he struck became evident. Mother Hope's witchcraft had brought back years to Leon. Though still bald, the rest of his body had returned to a younger version of himself. Not young, but younger — looking and feeling as he did in his late-fifties. Far better than feeling his actual late-seventies. In fact, Max could always gauge Leon's standing within the Magi organization, and with Mother Hope in particular, by how young he looked. At the moment, Leon looked quite well.

"Have a seat," Max said. "Let's talk."

As Max placed his arms on the table, Leon hesitated. Max knew that hesitation well — too many times in his life, he had been the one standing, trying to decide whether to give in and sit or not. He came close to making a joke in an attempt to put Leon at ease. But Drummond's voice in his head reminded him of the meeting's purpose. Making Leon comfortable would be an obstacle to that goal.

Max waited. He watched two students strolling towards the elevators — a young man and a young woman, both attractive, both ignoring each other as they stared at their phones. Before he could formulate a fully-sarcastic thought, the woman lifted her head and gave the man a playful shuck on the arm. They smiled at each other, kissed, and entered the elevator. The world changes; the world stays the same.

Leon finally dragged over a chair. Leaning his elbows on the table, he glowered.

Max said, "I appreciate you meeting with me today."

"Didn't have much choice."

"You've had plenty of choices, and you made the ones that led you to this point." When the words left Max's mouth, Leon flinched. Nothing more than a spasm of surprise but enough to give Max confidence. "Tell me what's been going on with the Magi lately."

"No." Leon leaned closer — perhaps trying to compensate for his momentary nervousness. "When you put this curse on me, you promised I wouldn't have to spy. I'm holding you to your word."

"I'm not asking you to narc. I didn't mean it like that. I merely wondered how things were going for you."

Locked in an expression of disgust, Leon said, "We are not friends and I've got no room to be pleasant with you anymore. The only reason I'm here is because of the pain you can bring to my life. Now, did you actually have something you need to talk to me about, or is this a pathetic attempt to intimidate me?"

Not the way Max had hoped things would go, but at least Leon knew enough to listen. No small talk, then. Probably better that way. He checked around the room once more, making sure nobody surreptitiously paid them any attention. Lowering his voice, he said, "I need you to get me some witch's water."

Leon squinted. His head dropped to the left shoulder. When his mouth opened, he erupted with a broad, strong laugh.

The students working at nearby tables glared at Leon. A librarian walked over and placed her index finger on her lips. Leon regained his composure and stifled his remaining chuckles. He had worked in this library in the past. He knew the proper decorum.

During this entire display, Max did not move a muscle. He kept his face serious, his body still, and his mind focused.

Lowering his eyes, Leon said, "You are either the dumbest, white fool I've ever met or you're looking real hard to die."

"I didn't ask for your commentary. I just need you to get me the stuff."

Leon looked behind him and at his sides as if expecting

some friends to pop out, pointing at him and laughing. When he looked back at Max, his face lost all mirth. "You're real serious?"

"I wouldn't have bothered with this meeting if I wasn't."

"It ain't going to happen. Mother Hope won't cast a spell to make witch's water. Not ever. It goes against all that she stands for."

"I figured as much, but she won't have to make it. For over a hundred years, she's been out there trying to control witches and put a muzzle on witchcraft. I have no doubt that in all that time she has come across witch's water more than once."

"If she did, she would've dumped the stuff as soon as possible."

"She can't. Pouring witch's water is what casts its magic. Once it's made, the only way to get rid of it is to use it. Plus, as I understand it, the stuff is very dangerous. Explosive. Not the kind of thing you're going to dump easily." Max held his eyes on Leon to underscore his next point. "Let's be honest. Whenever Mother Hope confiscated witch's water, she kept the stuff. She may have done so from the noble idea of keeping the dangerous water out of the hands of fools, but she also held onto it just in case."

"Just in case what?"

"Who knows? It doesn't matter. To a witch like Mother Hope, merely having the water is a form of power. And that's what she's all about."

With a dismissive utterance, Leon leaned back. "You don't know nothing. She's not in this for the power. It's the opposite. She does all she can to stop people from abusing magic."

"That's what you all say — you should make a brochure — but the evidence says otherwise. I can believe that she started all of this for good, but power corrupts — no matter how small or limited that power. She's not the same woman she once was."

With more pleading in his voice then he probably intended, Leon said, "You're asking me to betray her."

"Why the hell do you think we cursed you? We weren't

going to ask you to become better friends with her. Now we need you to find where she keeps this witch's water and bring us a couple vials of it. If you do it right, she'll never know."

"And I got swampland in Florida to sell you."

Max could sympathize with the position Leon found himself in, but sympathy only went so far. "Don't make me threaten you."

"I've never understood why you pick fights with her." Leon gazed up at the skylight. "Mother Hope and you are on the same side."

"She's been on her own side for a long time now."

"She's family to me."

Max had not intended to be drawn into a debate. He needed Leon to perform a task, and there was no room to negotiate. He heard Drummond in his mind nudging him to finish this conversation. Shut down all arguments and get Leon moving.

When he opened his mouth to follow through, he saw Leon's hand rubbing his chest. Max knew that feeling — at the location of the curse. Watching Leon made Max's own curse ache. He caught himself involuntarily pressing his hand against his sternum.

"I don't even have to tell you," Max said.

Leon glanced down at his hand against his chest. "I guess not." His mouth twitched, and he needed a long breath to wash away the hue of nausea crossing his cheeks. "I'll call you when I have it."

Leon left, and Max waited five minutes before also exiting. Walking back to his car, he pulled out his phone and called Sandra. He had done so out of habit, yet when she answered in mid-laugh, he remembered that she was with Peter at lunch.

"You sound cheery," Max said, crossing his fingers that any hint of jealousy did not seep through his voice. "What's so funny?"

"Oh, nothing. Peter brought up an old story, but you had to be there. It's not really funny. Just some stupid stuff we did as teenagers."

"I see." He cringed inwardly and commanded himself to get

out of this call fast. "I wanted to tell you that everything is set up with Leon."

"Good. I'll let Peter know that we'll be making some progress soon."

"Sure. You do that." Max cut the call and smacked his forehead. Idiot.

He went down stone stairs that led to a faculty parking lot. Across the street, the general parking lot. He stormed towards his car, his mind seeing nothing around him. He only heard Sandra's laughter.

What if Drummond was right? What if, despite Sandra's loyalty, Peter somehow drove a wedge between them?

Fumbling out his keys, he said, "Stop it, Max. You're being paranoid."

The attack came as he opened his car door. A large body pressed him up against the glass and two sharp jabs to his side followed. Max reacted without thinking. He twisted back, jamming his elbow into the head of his attacker. He made good contact, but not enough to free himself. The response came quick and brutal.

Two hands clasped upon his head and slammed him against the side of the car. The world spun and all sound muted. His balance disappeared, and a second later, he ended up sitting on the parking lot pavement.

He gazed upward, trying to get a view of his attacker, but the man — Max could tell now that he had been attacked by a large man — wore a ski mask.

Must be hot in there.

"Drop the case," the man said. "Drop it or your boy won't ever come home from school one day."

The man punctuated his sentence with a sharp kick into Max's leg. A flash of fire burned straight up into his gut. By the time Max's head stopped spinning, the assailant had vanished. Once he managed to get back to his feet, Max slipped into the driver's seat, caught his breath, and called J's school.

Pulling onto the road, he told them to have J ready to leave. He was on his way.

Chapter 13

MAX RACED ALONG SILAS CREEK PARKWAY, his muscles taut as he weaved through the Sunday afternoon traffic. Most of the churches had let out by then, and slow drivers filled the lanes. When two cars kept pace with each other blocking the way forward, Max pressed hard on his horn and spouted a handful of foul words.

Horrid images flooded his mind — J being kidnapped, tortured, and murdered.

As he neared the school, traffic mercifully thinned. Only a few students took classes on Sunday — mostly remedial students, but in J's case, it was a mixture. He was a smart kid, but he had missed out on several years of school while he lived as a homeless teen. He had catching up to do. His teachers recognized that he could advance quickly if given extra attention.

Max had often heard that teachers were the unsung heroes of the world, and J's teachers proved it. Two of them switched off Sunday afternoons to meet with the boy at school and privately tutor him. Max offered to pay them extra, but they turned him down. They said they could use the money, but they would get into a lot of trouble if they accepted.

Screeching to a halt in the parking lot, Max bolted from the car and dashed over to the building's entrance. Mrs. Ekman, one of the noble teachers, had J waiting in the lobby. When Max saw J, his heart jumped. Tears welled up and his chest tightened. Scooping J into his arms, he kissed the top of J's head and smelled his youthful skin. J squirmed away, pushing harder than necessary, and at first, Max thought he had been rejected. But upon seeing that no harm had come to the boy, his awareness widened. Several students stood in the hall watching. J glanced back, and Max just knew he looked at the cute girl on the end.

With a questioning frown, Mrs. Ekman said, "Is everything okay?"

"It will be now," he said.

Without further explanation, he ushered J outside toward the car.

They had barely reached the main road when J said, "Are you going to tell me what this is all about?"

Max had been so wrapped up in getting J that he had failed to give any thought as to what to say. His gut told him to be straightforward with the kid — J had spent enough time living on the streets that he wouldn't scare easy. Trusting his instincts, Max opened up and told J everything.

With one exception.

Max avoided those details of the case concerning ghosts and witches. Instead, he focused on the unknown, dangerous man threatening them. He justified this omission by the simple fact that if J thought the case involved ghosts, he might not take the threat seriously. However, Max's earlier conversation with Sandra echoed in his head — they were going to have to level with the boys. Soon.

"You know," J said, "you won't be able to keep me out of school forever. I mean, eventually this case will end, and you'll have a new case and a new threat."

"I can't let you be a sitting target."

"I don't want to be one, either. I'm just saying that we're going to have to figure out how to deal with this stuff because I want to stay in school, and if you think it's going to end after just this one time —"

J was right, of course, but Max had to focus on the present danger — he could worry about tomorrow's danger another day. Like a dashboard sensor lighting up to warn of an overheating engine, Max felt a rise in J's agitation. He had seen this before in both of the boys — a fight or flight response honed sharp from spending too long in daily survival mode. He needed to refocus J, and he had the perfect way to do it.

"Who was that girl you were looking at?"

J's attention shot forward — he didn't even dare glance at Max from the corner of his eye. "What girl?"

Max smirked. "Cute one on the end. Huge eyes, pretty smile, cornrows."

"Oh, that girl. Her name is Dalya."

"How long you been interested in her?"

"What?" J changed positions three times in his seat. "You're crazy."

"Okay. You don't have to talk with me about it. But if not me, who do you got? PB? He doesn't know anything more about girls than you do."

He gave J a few minutes to think it over. He watched the road, not wanting to pressure the boy.

At length, like a chick steadily cutting a hole in its shell, J said, "Yeah, I like her. I got no clue if she likes me."

Max stroked his chin, putting on a show of serious consideration. "Let me ask you — when you're going between classes during the day, is she there? Does she walk with you between similar classes?"

"Sometimes."

"And at lunch, does she eat nearby?"

"I guess. Sometimes she brings her friends over and sits with me."

"You ever have lunch with just you two?"

"Couple times."

Max nodded sagely. "She likes you."

J raised his eyebrows and gave a little shake of the head. "No way you could know that."

"It's the benefit of being much older than you. At your age, I would never have known it either. But, I'm telling you, I know what I'm talking about. When a girl finds excuses to be near you, she likes you. Otherwise, you wouldn't be seeing her around at all. She'd have every reason to never be near you, and especially, she'd never be alone with you."

"For real?"

"Look, it's simple. When you go back to school, see if she

asks you what happened? She saw me come get you. If she asks you about it, shows interest or even better, concern, then you know she likes you. If you still need convincing, casually drop that I'm going to pick you up for the next few weeks, so you'll be waiting by the outside benches at the end of every school day. Or wherever, it doesn't matter. Just make sure it's a place you don't normally stand. Then, you see if she's standing there hanging out with you. If she is, you'll have no doubt she likes you."

J twisted his mouth to the side. "I can't believe that's all there is to it."

"If it was more complicated than that, men and women would never get together."

J grew quiet, and Max listened to the shushing of wheels against the road. After a few minutes, J said, "It's always about the girls, isn't it?"

"Definitely."

By the time they parked in front of Mrs. Porter's apartment building, the tension had left Max's neck. In fact, if not for his bruised side, he would have been feeling quite relaxed. He walked J up to the third floor.

When Mrs. Porter answered the door, she gave J a hug and Max a questioning look. "Long story," he said and walked in.

The apartment was small but functional. While she had only been living there a short time, it already smelled of the house Max had grown up in. Memories of chocolate chip cookies crowded next to memories of late nights falling asleep in his mother's lap. But underneath it all, he caught a whiff of something medicinal — that brought memories of spankings, lectures, and groundings.

It was the same sour odor that followed him now as his mother took him by the arm and pulled him into her bedroom. She closed the door after making sure PB and J had settled on the couch to chat with each other. Turning back to Max, her face soured.

"I don't mind having them here," she said. "I want to be clear about that. Don't misconstrue what I'm about to say. I love them, and I'm happy to be a significant part of their lives, their educations, and their upbringing. But you and Sandra have agreed to take on this responsibility, and that means you need to start doing it. It's time to step up and do your job as their guardians. I won't live forever, and then you'll be in a hole if you don't know what you're doing. And if I can tell you anything — you don't know what you're doing."

Kicking the heel of one shoe with the other, Max said, "I'm sorry. We are trying. We've even talked about this very thing. I promise, after we're done with this case, we will sit down and figure this out."

He could not tell from his mother's face whether she believed him, but her actions at least told him that she would play along for now. She left the bedroom, and he heard her happy voice as she hugged the boys and discussed what each of them had studied that day. Max said his goodbyes, but the boys seemed more interested in laughing with Grandma then acknowledging his exit.

In a day that had been filled with driving all around town, Max's drive home seemed the longest. Each mile that brought him closer took him further away from the Sandwich Boys. They were receding in his rearview mirror and he feared the distance would grow so long that it could not be bridged. By the time he reached his house, his mother's warning had seared into his brain.

Pulling into the driveway, his mood worsened — Sandra's car was not there. He pulled out his cell phone and brought up her number. The pale light of his phone dared him to call her. He shut the phone off, got out of the car, and slammed the door hard.

Entering his house, the quiet struck him fast. The house was empty — no Sandra, no Drummond, no mother, no boys. Walking down the hall, his footsteps echoed in his ears as if he walked through a mausoleum.

He tried to do some research in his study, but his mind would not focus. Not on work, at least. He had no trouble focusing on Peter Rathburn dining with his wife.

Max paced from the kitchen to the living room to the dining room and back to the kitchen. When that failed to clear his mind, he climbed upstairs and paced from bedroom to bedroom. That failed him as well. In the end, he sat at the kitchen table, arms folded, and a scowl digging lines into his face.

Lunch had to have been over. Yet he knew his wife well, and if she had deviated from going to the office or coming home, she would have called or texted. Considering the threats made on his life and those made against J, Max could not help but worry that something had happened to her. He brought out his phone and pulled up her number again. He quickly put it away.

Nothing serious could've happened to her yet. If it had, the authorities would have contacted him by now. Even if the lunch had gone shorter than he thought, there would not have been enough time to take her against her will, kill her, and dispose of the body without getting noticed.

Max shivered at his macabre thoughts. No, she would be fine. If those who had attacked him wanted to hurt her as well, they would have threatened her instead of J.

Unless they used the threat on J to divert Max away from Sandra. That connected to another thought, one that had been brewing in his gut since Peter had called that morning. What if the real threat was Peter? What if his invitation to lunch had been merely a ploy to get Sandra out of the way so that Peter's henchmen could work over Max? It sounded plausible, except for the fact that Peter was not a movie villain with henchmen.

Five more minutes. He would give her five more minutes and if she did not call or show up, he would call her. If she got mad at him for checking in on her, so be it. And if she didn't answer the phone?

Then he would start calling hospitals.

Chapter 14

FOUR MINUTES AND THIRTY-ONE SECONDS LATER, he heard Sandra's car pull into the driveway. Unsure if he wanted to hug her or scream at her, Max stayed still at the kitchen table. The refrigerator hum kicked off leaving the room more silent than before.

"Max?" Sandra called as she entered the house. She walked down the hall and into the kitchen. Max did not move.

With a meek grin, she said, "I come bearing gifts." She held up both hands. In one, she held a bottle of wine — red, cheap. In her other hand, a bag of Wendy's drive-thru.

Barely moving his mouth, Max said, "It's going to take a lot more than a sentimental meal. Where have you been?"

"It was a long lunch, and afterward, we walked around the streets — window-shopping and chatting about old times. That's all."

"I'm sure it was. But that doesn't mean he didn't have something else in mind."

Sandra shoulders dropped. She set the wine on the table with a click and tossed the bag of Wendy's carelessly to its side. "I'm trying to be nice here."

"I know what you're trying to do. You feel guilty, and you're hoping that this gesture will make it all better."

Sandra set her jaw and her nostrils flared. She put both hands on her hips. "Now you look here," she said, her tone sucking away all of Max's anger, leaving him confused as to why he felt in the wrong. "You need to stop acting jealous."

"I'm not. Even if I were worried about him, I completely trust you."

"This is trust?" She sounded more like his mother than either of them would dare admit.

"I think Peter might be trying to cause trouble with our marriage."

Sandra pulled out a chair and sat, her anger narrowing into concern. "You think that? I thought our marriage was doing fine."

Suddenly uncomfortable in his chair, Max said, "Well, Drummond and I talked —"

"You're taking relationship advice from Drummond?"

The way she spoke not only shined a light on Max's foolish thoughts, but they also dismissed him with too much ease. Pushing his chair back on two legs, he said, "What did Peter want, then?"

Hiding her face, Sandra got up and grabbed two wineglasses from the cabinet. "He wanted what he said he wanted — an update. But we're old friends, so after the update we went on a little nostalgia trip." As she spoke, she focused on pulling out a corkscrew and getting to work on the bottle of wine. "If you want all your fears confirmed, then yes, I suspect Peter wants a closer friendship from me. But even if that were to happen, it's just a friendship. It has nothing to do with our marriage."

"I'm not saying that. I think our marriage is doing fine."

"Then what is this about?" She pulled out the cork, poured two glasses, and handed one to Max. Reeling in some of her bite, she said, "I promise you, there is nothing to worry about."

"I know that." He set his glass on the table. "This case has become more serious, and I don't know how Peter fits into it all."

"He's the one that hired us. How much clearer does it need to be?"

Standing, he took her wineglass away and set it next to his. He put his arms around her. "I was attacked today. Guy came along and punched the hell out of me. Then he threatened J."

"What?" Fire returned to Sandra's eyes.

"J's fine. He's at my mother's." Max went on to tell her all that had happened. "I've been worried sick about you. And yes, I was a little jealous."

"A little?"

"A lot. For now, we need to make sure we keep each other in the loop. You can't go away for hours and not check in with me. Not until we have gotten rid of this threat."

She rested her head against his chest, and he hugged her tight. Standing in each other's arms blanketed them with a field of security. They both knew it would not last long. Then Max's cell phone rang. Not long at all.

When he answered, he was surprised to hear the voice of Leon Moore.

"I got it," Leon said. "I got your damn water."

Chapter 15

ONCE MORE, MAX DROVE along Route 40 with Drummond floating in the passenger seat. After Leon's call, he and Sandra agreed that it would be best if she went to the firehouse and prepared to use the witch's water. The irony that he sent his wife back to the man they had just fought about rang in his ears, but he justified it all with a simple thought — the faster they got this finished, the faster he would be done with Peter Rathburn.

With a plan for the evening made, Max drove over to the office to collect Drummond. At first, the ghost refused to leave the bookcase. Max cajoled him with simple appeals to Drummond's vanity — mostly by admitting that the ghost's suspicions about Peter had borne out.

"Maybe now you'll stop doubting me," Drummond said.

"Don't count on it."

Max pulled off Route 40 to take 74 South towards High Point. Leon had insisted on meeting in a public place. He chose the Palladium theater — a multiplex sitting in the middle of a strip mall on a hill.

Drummond pursed his lips as he squinted out the window. "This stinks of a set up. He says he wants to meet in a public place but then he picks a movie theater where entering and exiting is controlled. It's also dark which defeats the whole point of being in a public place. What really bothers me is the fact that you met him earlier today, and suddenly he has the vials of witch's water. I don't see how he could have pulled that off in such a short time."

"It bothers me, too. That's why I'm glad to have my partner here with me."

Drummond stretched his arms behind his head. "So, you're

finally admitting how much you need me. It's okay. I understand. Sometimes we forget to value the important members of our team until we have to do without them. But I'm here now."

"Don't act modest on my account."

Pulling off the highway onto Eastchester Road, Max entered a well-developed area of High Point. Gas stations, strip malls, restaurants, churches — all spread out over several miles where concrete and grass fought for control of the land.

When he finally reached the movie theater, Max had internalized all of Drummond's concerns. Walking through the parking lot, every lone figure became a possible threat. He scanned the crowds, looking for the person who stood out, who did not belong.

Perhaps Drummond reacted to Max's nerves, or perhaps he simply knew what Max would eventually ask of him. Either way, he said, "I'm on it." He zipped ahead, passed through the walls of the theater, and scouted the inside.

Max bought a ticket — some cartoon about an ostrich that learned to believe in itself — and he entered the theater lobby. Drummond flew up next to him. The smell of fresh popcorn and fake melted butter drifted through the air along with the noise of kids, parents, and dating couples. Video menus displayed cartoon characters munching down on candy.

Drummond looked as if he had inspected a crime scene. "Back in my day, these places had a lot more class."

Max entered the men's room — bright, narrow, white-tiled — and chose a stall at the end. One man stood at a urinal and another washed his hands in a sink. Max closed the stall door and pulled out his cell phone. He texted Leon with his location.

With most of the movies in the multiplex starting within the next five minutes, Max expected the bathroom to clear out shortly. He heard the two men leave, and all remained quiet for a full minute. Then Leon entered.

Max stepped out to greet him, but Leon walked right by and pushed in every stall door.

"Nobody's in here," Max said.

Leon came back, his face balled up. "I told you things were intense before, but today, it all jumped up to a near-warlike situation."

Max rubbed his chest and knew Leon caught the motion. To deflect Leon's thoughts from using the curse to his favor, Max asked, "You going to give me details?"

"Ever since the Mobley coven made a run for power, Mother Hope has been extra cautious. Even with me. Just trying to get to see her for our basic, daily update is difficult. But when I got back to headquarters today, I saw more guards in the hallways than ever before. And they were packing."

"Is that why you wanted to meet in public?"

Leon checked the door before coming back once more. "I don't know what the Mobleys did or tried to do, but they haven't given up since that whole kidnapping business you were involved with."

"I wasn't involved with their kidnapping. They hired me—"

"I don't care. I'm telling you, this is all getting hot."

A thought hit Max that sunk his stomach low. "If Mother Hope has her guards armed and in greater numbers, then you didn't get the witch's water, did you?"

"Now you're acting paranoid. That's good. You need to be like that."

Max's eyes darted towards the door. It was the only exit.

Leon got a strange look on his face. "Where's your ghost?"

Wondering the same thing, Max called out, "Drummond?"

Drummond's head popped through one of the urinals. "Everything okay in here?"

Trying not to show the great relief he felt, Max said, "I'm fine. What are you doing?"

"What do you think I'm doing? I'm out here keeping guard. You don't think I'd let one of Mother Hope's goons go into that bathroom with you alone and not watch for more. I'd be a terrible partner, if I did that."

"Thanks." To Leon, Max said, "Let's get this done. Do you have the witch's water or not?"

"I told you I got it, so I got it. Normally, this would've taken me days to figure out how to steal it, but with everything hitting the fan right now, nobody was paying attention to the holding rooms."

"So while Mother Hope's doubling the guard on herself, she had to pull that guard from where she kept her stash of loot."

"If you want to be crass about it, then yes." Leon handed over two vials of clear liquid.

As Max pocketed the vials, he wondered if the recent attacks on him may have been about the power struggle between the Mobley Coven and the Magi. If so, then his short-term strategy would be to focus on his current case and ignore this other trouble brewing. In the long term, he would have to deal with these warring witches — not something he wanted to think about.

Leon's eyes drifted to the exit. "Is there anything more you want from me, or can I go?"

As an answer, Max walked out. Drummond floated in the middle of the hall, and when the ghost spotted Max, he swept in close.

"You took a long time. Everything okay?"

Max nodded and patted his coat pocket.

"Excellent," Drummond said. "You can tell me the details in the car. For now, I think we —"

Leon stood behind Max. "Damn. They're here."

Following Leon's gaze, Max spied two middle-aged women standing in line to buy popcorn. They gazed back, and one whispered in the ear of the other.

"They're with the Mobley Coven," Leon said.

"I've met the Mobley Coven," Max said. "Those two ladies are not part of the coven."

"You really think an organization like that is nothing but the core thirteen women? They have far-reaching fingers. They find ways to infiltrate all the major organizations and institutions. They're no different than the Magi — at least, in that regard."

Drummond tilted his head closer. "He could be right."

"Then let's find out." Max zipped up his coat as he strode into the lobby. The two women appeared more focused on

Leon, but perhaps they looked at something in his general direction instead.

A family of four crossed into Max's view. Tapping his fingers against his chin, Max had to make a choice — run for the exit or face these women.

A third idea came ... along with a devilish grin. With a high-pitched cackle, Max jumped at the family of four and knocked their popcorn bags upward. Popcorn sprayed into the air like yellow and white fireworks. As the father began yelling, Max skipped across the lobby and knocked down two of the cardboard stands advertising upcoming films. A manager and two employees rushed out from behind the concession stand, pointing at him and yelling further.

In the commotion, Max figured Leon would have found a way out. If not, that was the old man's problem. Max bolted for the exit, burst outside, and kept running until he reached his car.

"I've always thought you were a bit looney," Drummond snorted. "Now, I know it for sure."

As he drove off, Max noticed that the witches had not pursued him. "Looks like they weren't Mobley Coven. Or if they were, they didn't have much interest in me."

Drummond appeared in the passenger seat. "Whatever is going on with them, it's going to be ugly the day it all explodes."

"We've got our own load of ugly to deal with right now. You sure about this witch's water?"

"I told you this stuff is volatile, unpredictable. I'm not even sure that it can help. But it will work."

"You never said anything about unpredictable."

"See what I mean?"

Max drove off toward Winston-Salem, the setting sun, and the firehouse.

Chapter 16

A TRAFFIC ACCIDENT had shut the highway down to one lane. Max texted Sandra to say they were running late, but she texted back not to worry. When she went to the firehouse, everybody was out on a call. Only Owen Williams remained, and he showed no interest in hearing anything she had to say. She had been there for close to an hour and still waited for the firefighters to return.

By the time Max and Drummond cleared the accident — an unfortunate meeting between an eighteen wheeler and a Mercedes-Benz — they still had twenty minutes of driving left. When they finally reached the firehouse, another unfortunate meeting announced itself — they came upon a heated argument.

Max could hear the raised voices from outside. When he entered, he picked out his wife's tones with ease. Standing in the hall, only feet from the garage, Max found Peter and Sandra arguing with Chuck Williams and Captain Renner. Upon seeing Max, Chuck flapped his hand out. "Oh, that's just great. Now we've got you to deal with."

Sandra nearly flicked off his nose with her sharp fingernail. "Don't you talk to my husband that way."

Reaching across, Captain Renner put his hand over Sandra's finger and gently pushed down. "Miss, let's keep things civil."

Max plastered on a smile and gave his wife a gentle peck. "Sounds like were not all getting along here," he said. "What's the problem?"

Peter said, "When I told them we needed to use the kitchen tonight, suddenly nobody wanted to be helpful anymore."

"It's not that," Captain Renner said. "The problem is that things are going too far. We've indulged Peter's obsession with our ghost for long enough, but there is no way I'm allowing a séance in this firehouse."

"It's not a séance," Peter said, smacking his hand against the wall.

Mocking Peter's action by mimicking it, Chuck said, "I don't care what you call it. You aren't listening. We don't believe in this crap. Got it? And there's absolutely no way we're letting you go pouring witch's pee all around."

With a frustrated groan, Sandra said, "It's not that kind of water. It's like holy water except it's been given a spell by a witch."

"Is that supposed to make me feel better?"

"If you would listen to me —"

"Listen to this," Chuck said, and shoved Sandra back.

Everybody leapt into action. Max stepped in between Chuck and Sandra while Renner and Peter pushed Chuck backwards.

From a few feet away, Drummond said, "Give the word, doll, and I'll make it so he has a headache he won't ever forget."

Raising his hands high, Max said, "Everybody calm down."

Renner wrenched Chuck's arm behind his back and pressed him against the wall. "Are you going to be calm? Are you?"

Though he struggled at first, Chuck quickly relaxed. "I'm fine, I'm fine. Sorry. All this stupid ghost talk is getting to me."

"Go to your bunk and cool down."

Chuck followed orders, but he made sure to send Peter a nasty glare before leaving.

Returning to Max's side, Sandra said, "Can we all talk this through like adults?"

Captain Renner scowled. "There's nothing to talk about. I make the rules around here, and there is not going to be any kind of magic whatever-you-wanna-call-it going on in the kitchen or any other part of this building."

"We were hired to fix a problem here."

"No, you were hired to amuse us at Peter's expense. Some lighthearted hazing of the newbie — that's all this was."

When Sandra opened her mouth to argue further, Captain

Renner put out his hand. "We're not discussing this anymore. My men and women have to be clear-minded and ready to take on whatever call comes our way. I can't afford to have them all worked up over a ghost story."

"But —"

"I appreciate that you take what you do seriously, and I apologize if we've offended you on account of we do not take it seriously. But my job is clear and you people don't belong in here. Your presence is putting lives at risk and is making my job harder to do. I'm asking you politely, please leave. Don't turn this into something ugly."

Peter turned back to Sandra and Max. Like a politician on election night who sees his opponent's lead has become insurmountable but refuses to yield, he said, "Perhaps we can reschedule for another time." He offered his hand to Max, and after they shook, he gave Sandra a playful nudge on her cheek. "I'll text you."

Max and Sandra walked back to the car with Drummond trailing behind. Max wanted to tell Sandra not to worry, that they would find a way to solve this, but the words died in his mouth. When it came to solving cold cases, they had one clear advantage — they could talk to the victims. Without that, their chances for success were no better than the police.

Driving home in silence, Max noticed a lightness on his shoulders. The tension in his neck had dissipated. He felt bad for Holly Claypool, but if he would admit the truth to himself, part of him was glad to see this case move off into the distance. No more Peter Rathburn meant no more stress with Sandra.

Sandra's phone received a text. The shift on her face from frustration to elation told Max everything — they weren't done yet.

"It's from Peter," she said. "He says we're to come back after two in the morning. He'll get us into the kitchen."

"He's going to sneak us in?"

"Does it matter?"

"I'm not too thrilled with the idea of breaking and entering a firehouse, especially while the firefighters are sleeping one room over. Even more especially when we're going to be using unstable magic."

From the back seat, Drummond said, "Never mind him, doll. You'll do fine. But it wouldn't be a bad idea to get some protection."

"You're right about that." Sandra pointed to an oncoming exit. "Honey, we're not done for the night. Go to the office."

Less than ten minutes later, Max had parked the car on the street, and they charged upstairs to their office. Without even bothering to turn on the lights, Max crossed the room to the coffee machine. Sandra followed, took the time to turn on the lights, and pulled back the circular rug on the floor.

Drummond scratched his jaw. "I think I'll check out the Other one last time."

"Why?" Max said. "If you haven't found anything yet, what makes you think this'll be any different?"

"I'm no use here. This'll give me something to do while Sandra casts her spells. Don't worry, I'll be back before two."

Sandra smirked. "He's going to see his girlfriend."

As Max prepared the coffee, he chuckled. "That makes more sense. I should've known." To Drummond, he added, "Who is it now? You still hanging out with Miss 1800s?"

"I happen to prefer women closer to my own age. Not that there's anything wrong with an older woman, but the gal I'm seeing now died only three years after me. We talk the same language. And I don't just mean verbally."

"We don't need to hear anymore. Go to the Other. We'll see you later tonight."

Over the next twenty minutes, Sandra consulted several old texts she had acquired in the last year. Max sat at his desk and sipped his coffee. He observed her work like a doe watching a brazen fawn stepping out on its own — cautious and fascinated.

Eventually, Sandra typed up her notes, printed them out, and set them on the floor at the edge of the casting circle. From her desk drawer, she pulled out two blank, metal pendants — each one a small rectangle, smooth and silver.

Finally, she grabbed three white candles before kneeling in the center of the circle.

"I need quiet," she said.

"I haven't said a word. Or are you trying to suggest that I leave?"

"You can stay. I just want you to understand that once I begin, don't interrupt me. I've made wards before, but since we're dealing with a torn ghost, there's no real manual on how to do this."

Max mimed locking his lips and tossing away the key.

"Thank you, honey," she said. "I love you."

Max patted his heart and blew her a kiss. Her warm reaction electrified him more than any magic she could create. He settled back in his chair, sipped his coffee, and watched her work. Once she had finished setting up, however, most of her work consisted of meditation. Max closed his eyes and attempted to quiet his mind as well.

He was never good at meditation, though. The coffee didn't help, either. So, he dug out his notes and read over the case once more.

By the time Drummond returned, Max had convinced himself that as much as he wanted to be done with the case, he also wanted to know the answers. What had pushed Wade Johnson so far over the edge that he murdered the woman he loved? The woman that saved him? And what kind of magic had he dabbled in?

With her casting done, Sandra threaded the pendants with lanyard ropes. She handed one to Max and put the other around her neck. "I can't guarantee how effective this'll be, but it's better than nothing."

The metal felt warm against his skin, and Max wondered whether that came as a result of the magic or Sandra's touch.

Drummond said, "Whatever ward you put on that thing, it's not bothering me."

"It shouldn't," Sandra said. "You're not a torn ghost."

"Speaking of ghosts," Max said with a twinkle, "tell us more about Miss 1940s."

Drifting for the door, Drummond said, "Not a chance, pal, not a chance."

Sandra texted Peter to announce their short arrival as Max drove the car. Taking a suggestion from Drummond, they parked one block over from the firehouse. For a sketchy neighborhood, the street appeared empty and quiet.

Sandra's phone chimed. "Peter sent instructions."

Leading the way, she cut a path across two backyards, through a copse of trees, and finished at the side of the firehouse. Peter stood by an outside door that led into the kitchen. He motioned for them to hurry up.

Max stayed close to Sandra as they scurried through the door. Peter stepped in behind them and eased the door shut to avoid any loud sounds. Max found it funny — a few years ago, trespassing through people's yards and sneaking into a firehouse would have sent his pulse racing. This time, however, the whole thing felt casual and a little dull.

Of course, what lay ahead would be anything but dull. Now that he stood in the kitchen and watched Sandra clear off the table, the ward around his neck grew heavier. He hoped Drummond couldn't see the pendant bounce against his beating heart.

Peter hung by the door leading to the rest of the firehouse. His head turned back and forth between Sandra and the dark hall. "You're sure about this?"

"It's a little late to back out," Max said.

Sandra crossed over to Peter. "I know this is scary, and while I can't guarantee anything, I promise you that we are the best around for this."

With a shaky nod, Peter said, "It's all a bit more real than I expected. I'm sure that sounds stupid."

"Sure does," Drummond said.

Sandra snapped her fingers twice to get everybody's attention. "We need to stand in a circle."

As they took their positions, Peter asked, "Can we pray before we start?"

"This is witchcraft. Somehow I don't think that goes well

with the kind of praying you want to do."

"Oh. Right. Well, do you have a spell that can make sure we don't get a call while this is going on?"

"A call? You mean like for a fire?"

"If the dispatcher goes off, we'll be busted. Captain Renner is ticked off enough. He finds you all here, and I'll lose my job."

Max said, "We sort of figured you were putting your job at risk when you texted us to come back here. Maybe we should hurry up. The faster we get this done —"

"Right, right. Let's get this over with."

From his pocket, Max produced one of the vials of witch's water. He pulled off the stopper and handed it to Sandra. She gazed over at Drummond.

"All you have to do is pour it in a circle. Oh, and good luck."

Despite the trembling in her hand, Sandra stepped up to the table. She held the vial over the middle. As she dribbled the clear liquid in a circle, her free hand clutched her homemade ward.

Chapter 17

THE INSTANT SANDRA COMPLETED THE CIRCLE, a trail of fire ignited along its path. Max winced at the unnatural brightness and put a hand up to shadow his eyes. As the heat increased, so did the height of the flames. Peter rushed across the room and grabbed a fire extinguisher.

When he came back, Sandra seized his arm. "Don't."

"I can't let this place burn down."

"Look," she said, gesturing toward the fire. Though the flames intensified and dark smoke spewed out the top, nothing burned. The fire did not spread and the smoke did not push out the breathable air. "Welcome to the world of magic."

Peter's hands dropped and the fire extinguisher clattered on the floor. He looked toward the hallway. With his mouth locked open, he shambled over. Keeping his eyes on the fire and one ear cocked down the hall, his mouth widened like a dog seeing an elephant for the first time.

Pointing to his ear, he said, "I can't hear anything."

"It's okay," Sandra said. "The magic in this room has created a bubble of sorts. Nobody outside this room can see or hear or feel any of it."

Drummond said, "Only as long as the witch's water is in effect."

"I can't believe this," Peter said. "Is this real?"

Part of Max wanted to throw a comment or two Peter's way, but he tamped down his jealous desire to jab at Peter's waning confidence and focused on the task at hand. "Holly Claypool, can you hear me? Come to the circle. We are here to help you. Please, Holly, come to us."

As the fire licked the ceiling, a figure appeared as if made out of the flames. Her pale face reflected the light and shadow surrounding her. Her long hair blended with the fire. Her attention drifted from Max to Sandra to Peter and even to Drummond.

Wade? Her voice crackled and sputtered like the blaze circling her.

"My name is Max. I want to help you."

My darling, where are you? Her head wrenched to the side as if startled by a noise. *What are you doing here?* Tears streamed down her cheeks. *No. Please, no.*

Keeping a healthy distance from the fire, Drummond said, "Hey, sweetheart, listen to me. What is it you're seeing? Help us out. Tell us who killed you."

Killed? I don't want to die.

"We don't want you to die, either," Sandra said, taking a step forward.

Holly peered through the flames. *Kathy? Is that you? I don't understand. What is all this?*

"I know it's confusing, but trust me. Trust Kathy. I won't steer you wrong."

What do you want? I already told you — your secret — he should know.

"That's right. And if you tell me what you see, where you are, then I can help you. I can pay you back for keeping my secret."

Peter edged towards Max and whispered, "What secret is she talking about?"

Max shrugged. He didn't want to answer because he didn't want Peter to hear any shaking in his voice. The fire at the base of the circle surged, sending orange tongues straight up to the ceiling. Everybody stepped backwards.

Using his hat as a fan, Drummond said, "You may want to hurry this up. I'm pretty sure I made it clear this stuff is unstable."

"Holly, you've got to listen to me," Sandra said. "Tell me what you are seeing. Are in the laundry room?"

Holly leaned closer towards Sandra, but then her head wrenched to the side exactly as it had before. *You? What are you doing here?*

"Who's there? Who do you see?"

Wade. It doesn't have to be this way. I know the truth, and it doesn't matter. You should leave. We can be better.

Pressing against the edge of the table, Sandra raised her hands to shoulder height in an open gesture. Max moved two paces to Sandra's right — if he had to tackle her to stop her from reaching into those flames, he would. Thankfully, he saw Drummond slide closer to her left side. The old ghost would probably have a better chance of protecting her against a supernatural entity like Holly Claypool. Nonetheless, Max prepared to leap.

Sandra said, "Pay attention to me. Remember? It's me — Kathy. You are safe. Do you hear me? Nothing can harm you. Let's talk about my secret."

Kathy? Is that you?

"She's repeating herself," Drummond said. "We should stop. If she's caught in a loop like you said, then we might be adding to her loop. We might be making things worse."

"I can do this." Sandra's hands gripped the edge of the table.

Max reached towards her shoulder but did not touch her. "Hon, I think Drummond is right."

I promise. Your secret is — Holly wrenched her head to the side. *You? What are you doing here?*

"Come on, Holly." Sandra slammed her hand against the surface. "Just tell me who you're seeing. Who showed up?"

The next seconds happened faster than Max could think.

Sandra's jolting had caused the water to shift. Drummond pointed at the table and yelled, "Max!" Max did not understand what exactly had gone wrong, but he heard the fear in Drummond's voice. Muscle memory took over. He lunged forward, wrapped his arms around his wife, and let his weight drop them to the floor.

At the same moment, Holly stuck her head through the fire. In a voice loud enough to rattle the dishes drying on the counter rack, she screamed, *"You!"*

Flames erupted around her head like a lion's mane. She soared out of the circle and rose. Her fiery body spread across the ceiling.

Max rolled atop Sandra to protect her. When he looked up, he saw Peter dash across the room and pick up the fire extinguisher. With all the skill of a trained athlete, Peter rolled forward and safely landed on his back. He let loose, spraying the extinguisher foam upward at the blazing entity above him.

Whether this hurt Holly or not, Max could not tell. But it was clear that Holly was lost, angry, and panicking. Like a burning snake, she slid across the ceiling evading Peter's attack.

Drummond floated up to her height. "Look lady, there is no reason to be anxious. We're here to help you."

Holly shrieked. Fire shot from her body and slammed into Drummond. He flipped end over end straight out of the building.

Gripping his ward tight in one hand, Max stood and squinted up at Holly. "Don't do this. You were a good person."

With another glass-cracking scream, Holly sent a blaze toward the ground. Max dropped and covered his head, but he felt no burn. Intense heat, but no burn. When he looked up, he saw the same confused expression on Sandra that he wore on his own face. Then he felt the ward in his hand crack in two. He jabbed out for Sandra's ward — cracked as well.

"Oh crap," he said as he heard Holly screech again.

Thunder roared and the ground shook. An invisible force barreled into Max's chest, thrusting him backward. As he lifted his head, he had only time to reach for Sandra. But he was too far away. He watched as Holly became a ball of flames and slammed her burning being into Sandra's head.

All went still. All went quiet.

Chapter 18

NOBODY MOVED, and Max had the passing thought that perhaps Peter would break down and cry. Instead, the man found his voice as he glanced down the hallway.

Whispering harshly, Peter said, "You need to get out of here." He opened the door they had entered through.

Max crawled to Sandra's side. She had no burns, no bruising, no signs of trauma at all. But she was unconscious. Max slipped his arms under her and carried her towards the door.

"Get her to a hospital," Peter said.

"They won't be able to help her."

"Don't be an idiot. She's probably got a concussion. Maybe more."

"And what do I tell them when they start asking questions? How do I get them to take care of whatever physical problems they can handle when they will immediately assume I've been beating her?"

"They won't assume that. They'll just want to help her."

Max stepped outside. "They can't. No matter what you think, you've never dealt with anything like this before. Leave it to the professionals."

Peter grabbed Max's shoulder and pulled him back. "I won't let you leave with her, if you are not going to the hospital."

"Back off." Holding Sandra in his arms was the only thing keeping Peter's jaw safe from meeting Max's fist. "I don't care what your past relationship with Sandra was. You're a stranger now. Nothing more than a client, at best. You don't get a say in this." Over Peter's shoulder, Max glimpsed Captain Renner walking up the hall. "You may want to worry about your job security a little more right now."

Glancing back, Peter's eyes widened. "I thought he couldn't hear us."

"He couldn't. Not while the magic lasted. But after that, you better believe he heard you shouting at me."

"I wasn't shouting."

Captain Renner entered the kitchen, took in the disarray, and gazed up at the extinguisher foam dripping from the ceiling. "What the hell happened here? Who are you arguing with?" Stepping further in, Renner caught sight of Max. "I told you not to come back here. What's wrong with her?"

"Concussion," Peter said. "Possibly more. I'm trying to convince Mr. Porter here to take his wife to the hospital, but he's being stubborn about it."

"Bring her in here," Renner said. "I'll take a look at her."

Max shook his head. "Not necessary. I've got this."

"Listen to the Captain," Peter said.

"You should be taking the same advice," Renner said. "Let me help this woman first. But don't go thinking I haven't noticed the fact that you are the one standing here with this guy. You better have a good explanation for this."

Max stared at Captain Renner, then his eyes followed to Peter. He gazed out at the dark grass and the copse of trees in the distance. He could never run fast enough with Sandra in his arms. These two well-trained firefighters would catch him in seconds.

"I really hate to do this," he said. "Drummond? You paying attention?"

Drummond rose through the floor. "Was there any doubt?"

With a swift motion, the ghost plunged one hand into the back of each man's head. Renner's body stiffened like a corpse while Peter yipped like a small dog. They dropped to the ground, unconscious.

Rubbing his hands as if he suffered arthritis, Drummond said, "It's all clear ahead. Get her home."

Putting the night air into his lungs, Max hustled through the trees and across the backyards until he reached the car. He rested Sandra flat in the backseat and asked Drummond to hover near her. With his hands wet against the steering wheel and perspiration stinging his eyes, Max drove home — trying to go as fast as possible.

"How is she?" Max glanced in the rearview mirror.

"The same as she was a few minutes ago. Keep your eyes on the road."

After a short drive, Max came to the first of a series of traffic lights on Silas Creek Parkway. While stopped at a red light, he pulled out his cell phone and called his mother.

Her groggy voice answered, "What's wrong? Nobody calls at three in the morning unless something's wrong."

"Sandra's hurt. Get the boys and meet me at the house."

"The house? If it's serious enough to wake me at three in the morning, you should take her to a hospital."

"I can't." The light changed and Max pressed the gas. "It's all part of the case, and I can't really get into it right now. I'm driving. Just meet me at the house." He cut the call before she could respond.

Twenty minutes later, Mrs. Porter and the Sandwich Boys had Sandra stretched out on the living room couch. Max refused to give them specific details but warned that a hospital would put her in a vulnerable position. To his surprise, they accepted this without protest.

Mrs. Porter went as far as to say, "The poor dear. But I have to point out that when you get involved in dangerous work with dangerous people, these things are bound to happen."

PB promised they would keep Sandra safe. J backed him up, adding that they had seen enough around here to know that they could trust Max's judgment.

"Just keep your eye on her. If anything happens, if she wakes up — when she wakes up — call me right away." Max went upstairs and closed his bedroom door.

He paced the room like an angry lion waiting for its chance to attack. He kept seeing that ball of flame descend from the ceiling and smash into his wife. He could feel the heat each time he imagined that moment.

Drummond entered through the outside wall. "You need to

calm down. You need to think."

"You need to shut up."

"I see you're still wound up. Take it out on something. Punch your bed or throw a lamp into the wall or if you really want to feel some pain, you can punch me. Do anything you need to do, but get it out. Sandra's counting on you to save her, and you can't do that if your brain is spinning around pissed off that this happened in the first place."

With a raging yell, Max dropped to his knees and pounded his fists against the bed. When he finished, he did not feel better but some of the tension had released. Enough that his mind had cleared.

"All okay now?" Drummond asked.

Getting up to sit on the side of the bed, Max said, "What the hell happened in there?"

"I know as much about torn ghosts as you do. But that's what we've got to figure out. Let's be thankful Sandra is still alive, and let's get our heads working on the problem."

"That's what I'm trying to do. Stop giving me pep talks and start thinking with me." Max knew he spoke loud enough for his mother and the boys to hear him, but he didn't care for the moment. Even if he had, he could never have held back the anger he felt.

Moving through the bed, Drummond eased up a few feet to Max's side. "How about we go back to the office? If we look through Sandra's notes, I'm sure we can find a reference to whoever she spoke with about torn ghosts. Then all we have to do is talk to that person."

"Except most of what she found was from old books. She even said that the majority of the witches she spoke with didn't believe in torn ghosts. Thought they were a myth."

"Then we go talk to the witches. Every single one in town if we have to. Somebody knows something. We should start with Madame Yan. She's been the nicest to you — well, I think she favors Sandra."

"That's true," Max said, rising to his feet. "There is one witch who will know the answer — or, at least, how to get it."

Drummond swished directly in front of Max. "No. Not that witch. That's not a good idea."

"And I'm supposed to take idea judgments from you?"

"Go to Madame Yan. She's a safer choice."

"Crawling underground to see a witch that's half-insane is not a good use of our time. If Madame Yan knew anything about torn ghosts, if she could have had the remotest possibility of knowing anything, Sandra would have already gone to her. No, there's only one witch who knows the answers I need."

"You're being stupid."

"I'm the one trying to doing something useful."

"It doesn't take a genius to know that talking with Mother Hope is stupid."

Max grabbed a pillow and threw it at Drummond. "It was your shitty idea to get this witch's water in the first place."

"We were out of options. And if you remember, I was very cautious about this stuff. I warned you over and over how unstable it was."

"Oh, I see. We've reached the *I told you so* portion of this argument."

Drummond clamped his mouth as he rolled his fingers into a fist. With patient and deliberate delivery, he said, "We won't get anywhere by replaying today's events. If you want to help your wife, then you need to work with me and figure out what we can do. But if all you want to do is yell at me and blame me, then I'll leave. Sandra means too much to me to waste time like this."

Max turned away. He couldn't think with Drummond's accusing glare. Closing his eyes, he saw it all happen again — Sandra banging the table, the water circle disrupting, Holly Claypool taking over the ceiling in a blanket of flames, and of course, watching a ball of fire plummet into his wife.

"You're right," he said. "We cannot waste time. Like it or not, Mother Hope is the only person who can do anything for us right now."

Drummond whipped off his hat and threw it at Max. Even

as it chilled Max's skin, the hat vanished and reappeared on Drummond's head. "Mother Hope is not going to help us. You know that. What are you going to do? Ask her to fix Sandra when what caused her affliction was stolen witch's water? You remember — the water we had stolen from Mother Hope."

"I don't expect her to actually help us, but she knows the answer." Max stormed to the door. "I think I can beat it out of her."

Chapter 19

MAX PRESSED THE ACCELERATOR further down as he swept by a series of eighteen wheelers trying to make time driving through the night. He ignored the vibrations in the steering wheel when he exceeded 90 miles per hour. Even a light rain did not deter him.

"You can't leave now," his mother had said when he had bolted out the door. "Sandra needs you."

Blinded with anger, he didn't reply. Though part of him remained aware enough to hear PB assure Mrs. Porter that if Max had to run out, he did so in order to help Sandra. Max could not be sure that PB believed the words he spoke, but Max appreciated the effort.

As the car strained to reach 100 miles per hour, Max's teeth ground together in a grim smile. At normal speeds, it would take him roughly 40 minutes to reach Greensboro. If he could go a little faster, he would cut that in half.

"If you don't slow down," Drummond said from the passenger seat, "you'll end up spending an eternity stuck with me."

"I can handle it."

"Oh, sure. I forgot about all those years you spent as a Hollywood stunt driver." Drummond braced his hand against the dashboard though, of course, he had no need. "It's raining and dark. Do you really want the next time you see Sandra to be her watching you floating next to your grave?"

Max pushed the car harder. "Why don't you make yourself useful? Fly on ahead and see what kind of security I'll have to deal with in order to get to Mother Hope."

"You can't still be serious. Just turn this car around, and we'll sit down and figure this out."

"Nothing more to figure out. Mother Hope is probably the only witch around who even had witch's water. She's the only one who can tell us how to help Sandra."

"What do you really think you're going to do? She's not an idiot. You can't go in and talk about how *a friend* you know is in trouble and needs her help. And the moment you start talking about witch's water, she'll put it all together. Like you said, she's the only one who even had the stuff."

"I don't know." Max slammed his arm down on the rest between them. His cheeks were damp but he couldn't be sure if that came from tears or sweat — probably both.

"Your only other option is to be straight with her. Admit you had Leon steal the water. But that means you have to give up Leon. Could you really do that? And even if you could — which, let's be honest, that's not the kind of man you are — then what makes you think Mother Hope won't snap on that curse she put over you? She does that and it won't matter how good a driver you are. You'll still end up floating around here with me. Only you won't even be a ghost. You really want that? To be stuck somewhere between life and death?"

Max did not answer his partner. He had no answer to give. Stuck between life and death described his situation perfectly. While Sandra drifted in some witch-created limbo, so did he. No need for a curse to link them — love did the trick just fine.

Red and blue lights strobed behind him. A second later, the police siren rang out.

"Crap." Max eased off the accelerator and pulled over to the side of the road. He brought the window down, shut off the engine, placed his hands on the wheel, and waited.

The police cruiser idled behind him with its lights flashing. And he waited.

Three trucks he had passed earlier in the drive roared by on the highway. And he waited.

Gripping and releasing the steering wheel, he closed his eyes and strained to calm down. After all, even when he reached Greensboro, nothing would happen instantly. Whatever Mother Hope had to say, she would play her games for quite a while.

Except it did make a difference. Every second wasted put Sandra's life at risk that much longer.

When the cruiser door finally opened and the police officer finally strolled her way toward the car, Max had to fight the urge to reach into his glove compartment and dig out his registration. After all, as impatient as he felt and as sarcastic as he wanted to be, he recognized that the cop did not actually stroll. She approached with caution. She had pulled over a car blazing along the highway well past midnight — not the kind of situation she would expect to find a happy, suburban family in the car.

"License and registration," she said, placing the beam of her flashlight directly on his face.

Carefully, Max reached over and pulled out the paperwork. She inspected his license, then turned her flashlight on his face once again.

"Sit tight," she said, and walked back to her cruiser.

Max watched her through his rearview mirror. While he suspected a police officer would have trained for desperate moves, his hand slipped off the steering wheel and rested on his keys. How fast could she be?

Drummond said, "You turn those keys, and it won't matter what happens to your wife. If she survives, she'll spend the next several years visiting you behind bars."

"At least she'll be alive."

"And she'll blame herself the entire time."

With a frustrated huff, Max eased his hand back to the steering wheel. "What is taking her so long?"

"What is going on with you? I know you're worried, but you don't behave like this. You think maybe that attack on Sandra also did something to you?"

"My wife is maybe dying and you think I'm acting strange because I'm pissed off and anxious? If anything, I think you're the one acting wrong. Why aren't you all worked up?"

"I am. But I understand that it won't do her any good if I blow my stack and get myself in trouble. Like with the police."

"I guess you're a better man than me."

"All I'm saying is that if you focus, we'll do fine."

"Sure." Any time Sandra's life had been in danger, Max knew part of his rational mind flew away. But perhaps Drummond's observation had some merit. Perhaps this time, he felt the threat deeper. "It's just ... well, we've been through so much together. I think it's starting to get harder whenever a case turns dangerous. Especially against her."

"You two are very close. More than most married couples I've ever known. But you need to be her rock right now. Fall apart later."

"I know. It's been hard because it seems like were not as close as we used to be."

"Horseshit." Drummond leveled his serious accusation look upon Max — one he normally reserved for criminals caught in a lie. "I see what this is really about. Peter Rathburn."

"Now who's talking crap?"

"I'm serious. You've been jealous since he first showed up, rightfully so, but deep inside you knew you had nothing to worry about. Yet still you went on acting hurt and giving your wife a hard time. Now, you're feeling guilty."

"I'm not saying that I agree with that, but I will admit that many of our recent conversations have not been the most loving. And, yes, I feel guilty if those are the last conversations we'll ever have."

Peeking at his rearview mirror, Max watched the officer leave her cruiser and approach once more. She handed back his papers. Tapping the car roof with her knuckles, she bent forward, bringing her face into full view.

"Mr. Porter, I clocked you doing 104. That's a serious offense. That's the kind of speeding which costs you a lot of money, takes away your license, and if you're stupid about it, can wind you up in jail."

She paused and gazed at the highway as if weighing a difficult decision. Max didn't buy it. Whatever her plan, she already knew what she would do. None of those thoughts eased his roiling stomach, but at least his detective brain still worked.

"Normally, Mr. Porter, I would have called in another cruiser and had you arrested. But under the circumstances I find myself in, all I'm going to do is give you a warning."

Max had no clue what her problem was, but he didn't care. "Thank you, officer. I'll lay off the speed."

She chuckled without any sense of amusement. "I haven't warned you yet."

Keeping his focus straight ahead, Max could hear the threat in her voice and see her menace out of the corner of his eye. He stayed quiet.

"I'm giving you a message from Mother Hope." The police officer reached in, gripped Max's chin, and turned his head to face her. "She doesn't know why you're so angry but she says she can feel it in the air. She wants you to know that whatever you're mad about, she doesn't have time to deal with it tonight. Now, if that isn't clear enough, she wants me to let you know that if you keep driving to Greensboro, if you set foot near her, you won't ever leave. Is all of that clear?"

Despite her iron lock on his jaw, Max managed a nod.

"Good. A half mile up the road is an exit. You take that, turn yourself around, and go home." She ripped a piece of paper from her ticket book. "I'm only writing you up for eight miles over the speed limit. If I ever pull you over again, there won't be any mercy."

Max stuffed the ticket in his coat pocket. "Don't worry. I don't normally drive like this."

"You just do as I said. Don't make me have to escort you all the way back to Winston-Salem."

After the police officer returned to her car and drove off, Max started his engine and headed for the next exit. Between the rage prompting him to go after Mother Hope, the adrenaline coursing through him as he drove 104 miles per hour, and the gut-twisting nerve bomb of Mother Hope threatening him via a police officer, it amazed Max that he could calmly drive at all. He had been every bit the idiot that Drummond accused him of. What had he been thinking? Sure, he had been angry — still was — but he had no excuse for his rash behavior.

Snatching a glimpse of the ghost, Max knew to keep his mouth shut. Drummond gloated enough without any encouragement. Instead, Max took the energy prickling his bones and tried to divert it to something useful.

"I think you're right," he said, using these words to grab Drummond's attention. "There's no use in visiting a witch. Like you said, it's all a myth to them. Any constructive ideas on how we can help Sandra?"

The smirk wrinkling Drummond's cheeks dropped to become a thoughtful line. "Best thing I can think of, and I'm not saying this would work, but at least it's a place to start —"

"Spit it out."

"Whatever Holly's problem is, we need to help her move on. That's all a ghost ever really needs."

"You don't."

"I chose to stay. But most ghosts are stuck here because of trauma or a curse or, in the case of Holly, perhaps a little of both. Or maybe something else, I don't know. But that's the one place we know we can find the answers."

"And how are we going to do that?"

"When the case goes dead, you have to start from the beginning. Re-interview everybody you spoke with before. Go over the evidence again. Find the clues you've missed."

"I'm not sure we have time to get Joe Pardini or Floyd Claypool to talk with us again."

"It may be our only choice. We've got to solve Holly's murder. If we can find the truth of what happened and present it to Holly, then maybe she'll move on. If that happens, then all of the magic connected to her might move on as well — including whatever she did to Sandra."

"That's a lot of *ifs, maybes,* and *mights.*"

"You got anything better?"

Out of the depths of his head, an idea brightened. "What about Madame Yan?"

"The woman who lives underground like a mole? She's a witch."

"I know she's a witch, but we've always had good luck with her. She likes Sandra. She'll probably help us for that reason alone."

"Oh, I'm sure she'll help us. It's the price she'll make you pay that worries me."

"For Sandra —"

"Witches are a last resort. The very last. So far at the bottom of the list of things to do that you've got to stop thinking about them and start focusing on the task at hand. We rework the case, re-interview people if needed, go over the evidence. Real detective work."

Max pictured Sandra, saw her unconscious on the couch, and cringed. There had to be a better way than poking aimless questions at people who either didn't want to remember or were too happy to share a few hours. What he really wanted to do, what he knew would make him feel better and give him a sense of momentum, was research. Sandra often said that was his superpower. How useless if he could not think of a way to use it.

Wallowing in these thoughts, his mind wandered into picturing the fiery attack on his wife yet again. Holly had been surprised by the appearance of somebody. She kept saying it — *You? What are you doing here?* Something else she had said tickled the back of Max's mind.

"A secret," Max said. "Holly had mentioned that she knew a secret."

Drummond's hand went up to his chin. "That's right. She thought Sandra was somebody else. The person whose secret she knew."

"You remember the name?"

"Karen. I think."

Max snapped his fingers. "Kathy. It was Kathy. I can research a name. And that means we don't have to go running in circles over old interviews."

Drummond smiled. "Because now we have a lead."

Chapter 20

THE CLOCK ON MAX'S DASHBOARD READ 4:28 A.M. Circling the block around his office, he found one parking space open. As he hoofed his way to the building, the brisk night air helped wake him from the post-adrenaline letdown.

"This is probably going to take a while," he said to Drummond. "It'd be better if you went to my house and watched over Sandra. Come get me if anything happens."

"I'm not sure that's a good idea." Drummond kept pace with Max while floating in the middle of the road. "There's already been two attacks on you."

"Nothing I can do about that right now. And if you were here with me, you would be just as surprised as me if somebody took a sniper shot. Besides, you hate research."

"I wasn't planning on helping you with that part of it. Way I saw it, you'd hit the books and I would float around the perimeter. Keep an eye on things."

"I appreciate it, I really do. But they also threatened J. With Sandra in a vulnerable state, I would think they might see that as a ripe opportunity. I can handle myself tonight, but my mother and those boys are alone. Please, watch over them for me." Though Max had no desire to have Drummond bugging him for the next several hours, staring over his shoulder and asking questions, he also meant every word he said. He would work far better knowing his partner protected his family.

Drummond must have seen the sincerity in Max's face. With a strong and sure voice, he said, "You can count on me."

With the ghost on his way and dawn coming in only a few hours, Max knew the first thing he had to do when he entered the office — perhaps the most important. He crossed the room and prepared a fresh, hot pot of coffee.

As he listened to it purr and dribble caffeinated bliss, he slumped into his chair and ground his palms against his eyes. He glanced out the window and considered opening it up to let the cold air wake him further but dismissed the idea quickly. He needed patience — the coffee would do the trick.

While he waited for his laptop to boot up, his eyes fell to the casting circle on the floor. Sandra's casting circle. Powerless to stop the image of her assault from replaying in his mind, he rolled his chair closer to the circle.

"There is probably a spell out there that I could use to talk with you through the circle, but this will have to do. See, the thing is, as much as we have learned to talk with each other and to be honest with each other, sometimes I think were not very good at expressing ourselves. Hell, I'm a guy. The whole idea of expressing myself is still rather new. I know, I know — you'd point out that I was never one of those kinds of guys. But just because I wasn't completely cut off from my emotions, doesn't mean that I was completely in touch, either. Together, we've changed that. You've changed that. And I love you for it."

Axl Rose sang out the opening line of *Welcome to the Jungle* telling Max his laptop was ready for use.

Resting his eyes on the casting circle again, picturing Sandra smiling at him, he said, "I'm not sure what I'm trying to say. Not even sure why I'm trying to say it. Maybe, after having seen all the crazy things we've seen, maybe I think part of you actually can hear me. Or feel me. Perhaps by sending out these thoughts, I can give you something to latch onto. Because that's what you've got to do. I'm working at finding a way to help you, but I can't do it alone. You've got to hold on. Fight whatever is trying to drag you down. Do you hear me? I love you, and I'm coming for you."

He stared at the casting circle for another minute before he walked over to the coffee pot and poured himself a mug. Scalding his tongue, he greedily gulped too much coffee. But the instant jolt through his system made it worthwhile. After topping off the mug, he returned to his desk and got to work.

He had the name Kathy and the knowledge that she kept a

secret. He also knew that Kathy wanted to keep that secret from Wade Johnson. That suggested a relationship between Kathy and Wade. While not a certainty, Max thought it a safe assumption. Besides, if Kathy did not know Wade in any significant way, his job would be next to impossible.

Of course, there were a lot of ways to know a person. She could be Wade's sister, mother, grandmother, aunt or cousin. She could have worked with Wade. She could have nursed his wounds in Vietnam. She could even have been an ex-girlfriend. But the easiest and most practical approach would be to delve into his family.

For the first time since Peter Rathburn walked into their office, Max felt lucky. In less than three minutes, he had pulled up Wade Johnson's family tree going back two generations — and there she was. Kathryn Bryce Johnson, mother of Wade Johnson.

Armed with a full name, Max dug in to find all he could about her life. Born in 1932, Kathy grew up in Kentucky under the parentage of Samuel and Rebecca Barrett. Max could not find anything significant happening in her early years — no articles written to tell of her triumphs or failures, no online family biographies to share of her notable achievements, nothing. This wasn't unusual, most people lived quiet lives, but somewhere in this woman's history there was a secret bad enough to keep from her son.

At eighteen years old, she met Edgar Johnson when he came to town visiting a friend. According to their wedding announcement, Edgar became smitten with Kathy upon seeing her at a spring dance. Within three months, they were married. A few years later, after several tries, she gave birth to Wade. From all Max could uncover, it appeared that Kathy went on to live a traditional, nuclear family life.

Max tried several, more obscure avenues but could not find anything right up to Wade's death that appeared as a viable lead. He spent another half hour going over his notes on the case. Nothing.

Perhaps Drummond's idea of re-interviewing Joe Pardini

and Floyd Claypool would be the best way forward. However, Max thought it too early to call. The other problem — he had no leverage. Floyd had no interest in talking with him and Joe talked too much. Without real leverage to force the truth, both men would only serve to keep Max running in circles.

"Tell me you've got something," Drummond said as he slid through the wall.

Max jumped and knocked over his empty coffee mug. "Don't do that."

"How much of that stuff have you had to drink?"

"Enough to keep going. How's Sandra?"

Drummond lowered his head. "Not good. She's running a fever and mumbling."

Getting to his feet, Max said, "Other than knowing Kathy was Wade's mother, I've got nothing. I'm going back to the house."

"There's nothing for you to do there."

"I can hold her hand. I can be there for her."

"Come on, Max. You can't give up."

"I'm not. But I'm not getting anywhere here, so I might as well think while sitting by her side."

Max strode out of the office, hurried down the stairs, got in his car, and drove carefully home. Too much coffee, not enough sleep, and a speeding ticket in the glove compartment kept him focused on the road. When he entered the house, a pall in the air knocked the wind from his lungs.

Mrs. Porter rushed over to him, clasped his hand, and tugged him into the living room. The boys knelt at the side of the couch. Sandra's skin paled even as it glistened with her sweat. A beige washcloth rested on her brow.

"We're doing our best to make her comfortable," Mrs. Porter said. "I really think she should go to the hospital."

"They can't help her. Besides, I already told you, it's too dangerous."

"Staying here isn't doing her any good."

"I'm working on it. Your nagging won't make it go any faster."

"Fine, fine. If you know all the answers, then pretend I didn't say a word. I'm sure your knowledge of medicine far exceeds all those doctors at Wake Forest Baptist. After all, they've only had years of medical training."

"This isn't a medical problem."

"Sure looks like one to me."

Max brushed past his mother and sat on the edge of the coffee table. With his elbows on his knees, he brought his face close to Sandra. "Stay strong, hon," he whispered.

PB rested a hand on Max's back. "Don't you worry about her. She is strong. I mean, yeah, I know I barely know her, but it still hurts to see her like this. I mean, I don't know where she's from, her parents, nothing, yet she's like a mother to me. You know?"

"I do."

J said, "Same is true over here. Sandra is real tight-lipped when it comes to her family — I've never heard talk about a brother or sister or parents or grandparents or anything like that — somehow that don't matter. She makes us feel like we're part of a bigger family."

Max put an arm around each boy and pulled them in. He held him tight as he inhaled their scent. Their youth, their optimism, their strength — he tried to embolden his own resolve through them.

"When she's better," Max said, "we can all sit down together, and she'll tell you her whole family history. She's got a lot of cool people to talk about. She's had family in this country going back centuries. In fact, she's ..."

The boys looked at him. "She's what?" PB asked.

Max barely heard the question. His mind fired off thoughts with furious abandon. He had looked into Kathy Johnson's life but his focus had been on her role as Wade Johnson's mother. He never looked too far into her personal history and those that led up to her existence.

"Boys, there is no doubt that I am tired. I made a stupid error." He stood and stretched his arms. "You guys may have just given me the key to solving this case and helping Sandra."

"Hey, that's what we're here for," J said, puffing his chest.

Mrs. Porter, however, did not look impressed. "You are not thinking of leaving again, are you?"

"Of course not." He lied. "I will have to do some work in quiet. I'll be in my study. That is, if you don't mind staying and continuing to watch over her." Taking his mom's hand, he said with a mixture of sincerity and buttering up, "Knowing you're here, knowing her life is in your hands, gives me the peace of mind I need to do my job. Please, I need you."

Smoothing her blouse, Mrs. Porter fought to hide her grin. "Of course. I would never leave you in trouble. I'm your mother. Sacrificing my day for you is what I'm built for. Don't give it another thought."

Max gripped his mother's shoulders and planted a big kiss on her forehead. He dashed down the hall to his study. A familiar tingle grew in his head. He knew this avenue of research would prove fruitful. All his years of experience promised as much. Newfound energy surged through his body, waking him up, and echoing in his mind that this would be successful.

It had to.

Chapter 21

MAX SPENT TWO HOURS tracing Kathy Bryce Johnson's family tree. By going through census records, online posts of family members searching to connect or reconnect, marriage announcements, obituaries, change of name requests, and more, Max traced the various branches of her family back to the early 1800s. That was where he found his answer.

Stretching his legs, he meandered into the kitchen, poured a cup of coffee and popped two slices of bread into the toaster. When finished, he took a plate with the toast outside onto the backyard patio. Enjoying his breakfast with only the singing birds in the crisp, morning air, he went over the details in his mind and attempted to plan his next move.

Less than five minutes into his thoughts, Drummond manifested at his side. Max tossed his toast crusts into the yard and watched as three chick-a-dees flew down to grab the prize.

"How do you do that?" Max asked. "How do you know when to appear?"

"You're only asking me that now? I figured since you never bothered to ask, it didn't matter to you. You accepted it as one of my many gifts."

Max sipped his coffee. "If you don't want to tell me, that's fine. I was curious, that's all."

"Oh, relax. I don't have any special ghost sense for that kind of thing. I just figured you wouldn't need more than a couple hours. Am I wrong? Are you still face-planting the books?"

Glancing over his shoulder to make sure the sliding glass door was closed and that his mother would not overhear, Max said, "I got it."

Drummond brought his hands together in one loud clap. "Fantastic. What's the secret?"

"It's her name."

"Her name? What's so special about Kathy?"

"Her last name. That is, her family name going back far enough. See, Kathy's bloodline makes her a direct descendent of the Lewis family."

Drummond squinted. "Lewis? That sounds familiar."

"It should. It was connected with one of the most famous murders in North Carolina. Naomi Wise — a sweet, young orphan murdered in the spring of 1808."

"That's right. People called her 'Omi."

"There've been stories written about her, books based on her murder, several songs about her, even one by Bob Dylan."

"Okay, so Wade's mother is related to Naomi Wise somehow. Why is that important?"

Max leaned his elbows on the railing and inhaled the morning air once more. "To understand that, you need to know the full story of Naomi Wise."

Pushing back his hat and shaking his head, Drummond said, "Somehow I knew you were going to say that. Fine. Out with it. But let me remind you that your wife is suffering inside that house behind us. The longer you take with your story, the more she's going to suffer."

"I know that." Max held his focus on Drummond until the ghost recognized the seriousness in his eyes.

"Sorry. I know you're more aware of Sandra's situation than anybody."

"I need you to pay close attention. The point of this story isn't just the final conclusion. That part's important, but there has to be other important details that I'm missing. You understand? This story connects directly with Holly Claypool's murder. But I can't tell her this because she already knows it. She already knows Kathy's secret. There's something else in here that I'm missing, and it's the most important thing."

Drummond coasted in next to Max. "I'm paying closer attention to your words than I ever have before. Let me hear the story."

Closing his eyes to gather his thoughts, Max took a

meditative breath. He had to get this right. "This took place not far from here in Randolph County. Back then, it was all farmland. It took hard-working people to settle that land. One of them was David Lewis. Supposedly, he came to North Carolina running from the law in Pennsylvania. He had several sons, and they quickly earned a reputation — handsome boys but with nasty quick tempers.

"One of these boys, Richard, ran into some trouble with his brother Stephen. It's a convoluted story but the main point is that because of a misunderstanding regarding Stephen's wife, the two brothers had it out with each other. For the Lewis family this meant guns. It also meant that Stephen ended up murdered by his brother. Due to some legal wrangling, Richard was exonerated on a self-defense plea. After that whole mess, he moved upward to Guilford County, built a house on Polecat Creek, and had a son. Jonathan Lewis."

"I know that name," Drummond said. "He's the one, right? The one who killed Naomi Wise."

"Yeah. But let me get through this. We'll reach that part soon."

"Sorry. Go on."

"Jonathan was clearly a Lewis man — handsome and confident and quick tempered. Now, Jonathan had business in Asheboro and regularly rode his horse between the towns. On his route, he always rode by the Adams farm.

"Mr. and Mrs. Adams had adopted Naomi Wise. They had raised her well, if a bit sheltered, and she learned to work hard on the farm. Every description of Naomi Wise said that she was a handsome woman with charming eyes and soft, winning words. Most of her work centered on the kitchen but she had been known to wield a hoe in the fields when necessary.

"So, you can see where this is going. Nineteen years old, vibrant, beautiful, a real catch. And she's out working on this farm while Mr. Handsome rides by on his horse — they were, in a way, destined for each other. Every time John Lewis rode by the farm, he found a reason to stop. It was suggested that Naomi even began to collect things to furnish their home once they were married. Pots, dishes, even a bed."

Drummond snorted. "I believe they call that putting the cart before the horse."

"It was the world she lived in, or at least the one she believed she lived in. As for Jonathan, I don't know if he ever felt the same towards her. I suppose he cared about her, but perhaps he was looking for a good time and nothing more. It's difficult to tell from the various accounts because at this point, his mother comes into the picture.

"Descriptions of her tend to use words like *calculating* or *manipulating* or *ambitious*. You get the picture. She did not like the idea of Naomi Wise for her son. In fact, she had her eye on Hettie Elliott. Hettie was the sister of Benjamin Elliott who was Jonathan's boss. Now, Hettie would have been considered quite a catch at that time, but she was apparently not anywhere close to being in league with Naomi Wise when it came to beauty. Mothers being mothers, she forced her son to pay attention to Hettie. Being the dutiful son, he did as told. Apparently, this courtship went in a rather by the numbers way, and Jonathan had the decency to break things off with Naomi. However, he did not have the decency to tell her. He simply kept riding by the Adams farm without stopping and so did not see her again.

"This part gets a little strange. Naomi is heartbroken and starts crying. That doesn't seem to warrant what I'm about to say, but as I understand it, somehow the story of Naomi and her mournful weeping for this lost romance made its way as far as Asheboro and in particular as far as Hettie Elliott's ear."

Drummond said, "Nothing strange about that. It's not like people had radio or television back then. The ol' rumor mill was the central source of entertainment. I'm sure by the time Hettie heard about John's old love, that tale had grown well out of proportion."

"Oh, definitely. She heard that John and Naomi were engaged. John made a big scene about it, denying the engagement, and whatever words he used, he satisfied Hettie. But something must've clicked inside of him. I'm guessing that

Hettie's jealousy brought out a less attractive side of their relationship. It got John thinking that maybe this isn't the woman for him."

"You're wrong there," Drummond said like a man preparing to school a boy. "From what I'm hearing, it's clear to me that Jonathan Lewis felt something strong for Naomi Wise. The only reason he's hanging out with Hettie is because his mother made him. But then here comes this rumor that the woman his heart lives for is so upset and crying so much that word is spreading everywhere, well, I think that did something to him. Maybe hurt his heart. Maybe woke him up. Got him thinking about his future and who he wanted to spend it with."

With a grim grunt, Max said, "I wish that were true. And maybe it was for a very short time. Because, you see, after this whole dustup with Hettie, John began stopping at the Adams farm again. Sometime in the spring, and the records are unclear as to exactly when, Naomi left her house with a water pail and never returned.

"Now, a few miles south of the farm was a section of Deep River where there was a grist mill and a farmhouse right upside the river. A widow lived there — Mrs. Ann Davis. The evening Naomi disappeared, Mrs. Davis sat outside with her sons when they heard a horrible scream that suddenly choked out. The sons ran down to the river but couldn't find anything.

"Back at the Adams farm, Mr. and Mrs. Adams fretted over their daughter's disappearance. Unable to sleep, they rose early the next morning and searched for her. They found Naomi's water pail by the spring and tracks that led to a stump. Prints from horse hooves marred the ground on the opposite side of the stump."

Digesting every word, something Max had not seen Drummond do often, the old ghost said, "Naomi met up with somebody and used this tree stump as a step to get on top of a horse."

"That's what Mr. Adams thought. He sent word out and formed a search party. They followed the horse's tracks all the way to the Deep River ford. When they got there, they found the Davis family who told them all about the scream they heard in the night."

Max had uncovered a direct account of that moment in which an unnamed author had the foresight to take down the woman's words. According to this record, Mrs. Davis said:

> *Ah! Murders been done, sich unyearthly screams can't come of nothing; they made the hair rise on my head, and the very bloodcurdling my heart. O! Ef I had been young as I once was, I would a run down there and killed the rascal afore he could a got away! What is the world a coming to?*

Shortly after Mrs. Davis's declaration, several men discovered a body half-submerged and tangled amongst the weeds near the shore. Her heavy skirt had been thrown over her face, and her pale throat bore the distinct bruises of strangulation. Once the coroner had a chance to examine the body, he not only gave the official means of death as "drowned by violence" but also added a key detail — Naomi Wise had been pregnant.

"Sounds to me," Drummond said, "like Jonathan Lewis didn't have much time left in his life. I remember my mother telling me stories about people like George L'Estrange."

Max shrugged. "Is that name supposed to mean something to me?"

"He was a guy here in North Carolina back in the 1700s. Somebody seduced his sister and left her pregnant in the lurch. George hunted the guy down and filled him full of buckshot — enough to kill the guy. Even though there was a trial and George was found guilty of manslaughter, the locals took good care of him throughout the trial. It's rumored that his jail cell was furnished with comfortable chairs and a soft down bed. The governor even pardoned him. Point my mother was trying to make was that North Carolinians had no problem killing a man, if it's for the right reasons."

"I'm guessing Jonathan heard those stories too. He went running right away."

In fact, Max read an account of Deputy Robert Murdock who interviewed Jonathan's mother. She had no idea they were talking about Jonathan when she divulged that he had come home late that night with wet clothes. He claimed that his horse stumbled during a river crossing. She gave it little thought nor did it bother her that Jonathan quickly changed into clean, dry clothing and rode off that same night.

Murdock's investigation took him to the home of Colonel Joshua Craven. His wife said that Lewis had knocked on her door early that morning — around the same time Naomi Wise's body was being discovered. Mrs. Craven was quoted in court testimony as having joked, "What's the matter, Lewis, what have you been doing? Have you killed 'Omi Wise?" Lewis reacted poorly. Enough so that Mrs. Craven remembered the encounter.

Following Jonathan's trail continued to prove easy. He had no trouble learning that Jonathan went to an auction sale. Those that saw him there thought he behaved unusually. "He seemed reserved, downcast and restless." Not at all like the arrogant young man that they all knew.

"At this point," Max said, "he apparently showed interest in a young gal named Martha Huzza. Supposedly, he left the auction by escorting young Martha to her home. So, Murdock went to the Huzza's home. He walked in and found Jonathan Lewis sitting in a chair with Martha upon his knee. He surrendered without any further fuss."

Upon being locked up in an Asheboro jail, Jonathan Lewis claimed innocence. Over and over. People gathered outside the barred windows of his cell and threatened to rush in, take him out to the public square, and hang him. They figured it would save a lot of time and money.

"Especially because the State's case was built entirely on circumstantial evidence. Damning circumstantial evidence but they had nothing directly connecting him to Naomi. I mean, there was no way he was getting out of this — the hoof prints found by the stump exactly matched his horse, they found hairs on Naomi's skirt from when she rode that horse which, of course, matched in color — but without any witnesses or a weapon linking Jonathan to the murder, a good defense lawyer would be able to string along the case for some time. More than the locals wanted to wait."

This next part, Max had difficulty finding details on, other than verifying that it had happened. Apparently with the aid of some unknown persons, probably family, Lewis escaped prison. He disappeared, and this time he left behind sparse clues.

"Little by little, the rest of the family moved out of the area. Nobody wanted them around, and I doubt they were made to feel welcome. The Lewis family planted new roots south of the Ohio River and about six years later, the rumors were that Jonathan had married, had a son, and lived on the family compound."

Drummond clicked his tongue. "There's no way these people are letting that go."

"That's right. A meeting was held, and three men were sent to find and arrest Jonathan — Sheriff Isaac Lane, he's the one who deputized Murdock; George Swearegain, a young and strong man who could provide muscle; and none other than Colonel Craven."

"He was probably still pissed off about Lewis involving his wife in all this."

"They hunted him down, caught him, lost him, re-caught him, and marched him back to Randolph County. This time he couldn't escape. Probably tried but he failed. The whole thing went to trial, all the evidence was presented, the testimonies were given, and in the end — and this part is missing from the court records — somehow, Jonathan Lewis was found innocent."

"Are you kidding me?"

"A white man in the South in the early-1800s — he could get away with a lot."

"He probably bribed them."

"I thought that, too, but apparently he didn't have much in the way of money. Didn't really matter though, he died about four years later. Got sick and croaked. And that's when the final rumor made its way through the county. On his deathbed, he supposedly confessed to his crime. He said that Naomi pleaded with him to marry her and that, when he ignored her, she threatened to ruin him and any chance he had of marrying Hettie Elliott. He agreed to meet with her that night. He came by on horseback and said that he had come to marry her. She mounted the horse so that they could ride off to the local preacher straightaway. He then took her to Deep River and strangled her. During the struggle, he had pulled her skirt over her head to muffle her screams. He threw the body in the river and began his clumsy escape."

Max finished his coffee, arched his back, and groaned. Drummond took off his hat and gazed out at the yard.

"Is that it?" Drummond asked. "Don't get me wrong, you tell a long story, but you asked me to pay attention and I did. How does any of this link up with Holly Claypool's murder?"

"Because Jonathan Lewis had a son and they were living in Kentucky. Wade's mother, Kathryn Johnson, is a direct descendent of that line. Which means that so is Wade."

"Hold on. Are you telling me that you think Kathy's big secret was that her great-great-great-grandfather was a notorious murderer, and that somehow this led to Holly's death? Look, I know you can make some brilliant intuitive leaps, but I'm thinking this one may be a leap too far."

Keeping his voice calm so as not to wake his mother or the boys, Max said, "You don't think there are a ridiculous number of parallels? A member of the Lewis family, a violent man, seduces a sweet, innocent, young girl and then murders her partially by strangling her."

"I admit there are a lot of similarities but —"

"I know it sounds strange, but we're in the business of strange."

"Fine, but say this is the big secret — who is really going to care almost two hundred years later?"

"A lot of people. When it comes to something like this, North Carolina doesn't forget. Not only have there been songs written about Naomi and stories published and mothers telling their sons about it in one way or another, but in 1879 — that's seventy-one years after the event — a cotton mill was built at that old ford of Deep River. You know what they called it? Naomi Factory. Since then, the town of Randleman was formed in that area which brought with it Naomi Falls and even the Naomi Methodist Church. Even today, you can find online groups of people who believe they are Naomi Wise's descendants — a tough call considering she was an orphan. But that doesn't stop people. So, I don't think it's so crazy nor too much of an intuitive leap to think that in 1973, this whole thing happened again."

"I'm still not convinced, but I'm willing to listen. What is it you think happened?"

"Best as I can figure, somehow Holly Claypool found out about the Johnson's connection to the Lewis family. I think Kathy begged Holly to keep it a secret which suggests that Wade didn't know."

Drummond nodded. "You think somebody told him, not Holly, and he felt betrayed by her. Maybe he followed John Lewis's lead and set up a secluded meeting with Holly. He confronts her, loses his cool, and strangles her. Distraught over what he had done, he pulls out his gun and takes his own life. I suppose it could've happened that way, but that doesn't explain the casting circle symbols in the newspaper photo. And it certainly doesn't explain why she ended up torn ghost."

"That's why I cross-referenced those symbols with some of Sandra's books. Here's what I think happened."

The snap of a branch coming from within the tree line broke the morning quiet. Max and Drummond both perked up like deer.

Drummond said, "Somebody's watching us."

Chapter 22

MAX SAW A SHADOW MOVE between two trees. Snapping his fingers back at the house, he said, "Watch Sandra. Don't take any chances. If somebody comes in for her —"

"They're dead." Drummond shot through the wall with a dark, determined countenance.

Launching onto the grass, Max sprinted for the trees. He heard the crushing leaves as his target sped off. Once Max broke into the woods, he had to slow in order to avoid tripping.

Off to the right, he saw movement. Dashing around a thick trunk and hurtling a small deadfall, he made his way toward what he thought to be his enemy. But it was only a large rock.

Breathing hard, he scanned the woods. Nothing. Tree after tree, one looking much like the next, and no hint of motion amongst it all. He closed his eyes and strained to listen — perhaps he would hear hard breathing or a kicked stone. But nothing.

With his pulse calming, he turned back toward the house. The fresh scent of the woods reminded him of being a kid and running around with his friends playing soldier. That made him think of Wade Johnson, a real soldier. And that led his thoughts back to what he suspected had really happened the night of Holly Claypool's murder.

Holly had learned of Kathy's past, and while she respected the need to keep it a secret, she also wanted to be honest with the man she loved. The idea of marriage had to have come up between them, and she could not see how they would have success if they began their journey together with a lie at the foundation. So, at the risk of forever angering her future mother-in-law, Holly told Wade the truth.

He may have denied the whole thing or acted like it did not

matter, but Holly knew better. She understood that many of the families in North Carolina had long memories. Somehow — and Max felt fuzzy on this part — Holly got it in her head that if they could simply summon the spirit of Jonathan Lewis, they would be able to show people that Wade was not like his ancient relative. Or perhaps she thought a spell would be able to clear the Lewis name. Whatever foolish notion drove her, Max could see that the idea was doomed from the start — people wouldn't care at all. Hatred toward the Lewis family ran deep and no amount of charm, decency, or logic could change that. Besides, Holly's plan lacked all three.

That night, Holly and Wade met with their naïve purpose in mind. Whether she knew family members who were witches or bought the information from an untrustworthy source, she had a basic summoning spell at her disposal. The symbols she drew matched a spell used to communicate with a ghost already in the room. At least, that's what Max could derive from Sandra's cryptic texts. It would never have worked in bringing someone like Lewis back from the depths of wherever he resided.

Somewhere in the middle of the casting, they were interrupted. Holly looked at the intruder and said, "You? What are you doing here?" Kathy Johnson walked in, angry at this betrayal of her confidence, and disrupted the casting — perhaps wiping her hand across the circle, knocking over the candles, or even shoving Holly out of the way.

The result was catastrophic.

As Max returned to his house, he wondered how close his supposition matched reality. His story appeared to connect with the facts they had, but his gut told him that he still missed some crucial details. He really needed somebody like Sandra. Someone who understood and believed in the idea of a torn ghost.

Max entered his study and collapsed in his chair. Drummond flew through the wall.

"Did you get him?"

Max raised an eyebrow. "Does it look like it?" Before the two could launch into a morning battle of witty remarks, he added, "This guy is really bothering me. He doesn't make any sense. The first time he comes after me, he's shooting at me, trying to kill me. The next time, he jumps me in a parking lot, beats me up, threatens me, and then walks away. And now, he's just lurking in the woods. Why would somebody threaten me in reverse? These things usually escalate, not the other way around."

"Yeah, I've been wondering that myself. It certainly suggests that he wasn't trying to kill you the first time. Merely wanted to scare you. I'm also thinking that we're dealing with an amateur. He came in hard at the start, harder than necessary, and when that didn't frighten you off, he didn't know where to go. Maybe even scared himself with the reality of what he almost did. So, he decides to jump you. That didn't work, either. If anything, it got you working harder on the case."

"You think the threat on J's life is just more bluffing?"

"Without a doubt. The boys are going to be fine. This last time proves it. He's watching you, keeping an eye on you, but he doesn't know what to do about you."

Max frowned. "If he's getting weaker with each try at me, why do you sound worried?"

Staring out the window, Drummond watched the tree line. "Because a guy like that is unpredictable. Worse, he's been made to feel ineffective. I think he'll come after you again, and it might be in a big way." He turned to face Max. "He's not going to make an attempt on your life, but he'll try something reckless — maybe more reckless than shooting at you with a sniper rifle. Perhaps he'll try to stage a mugging or robbery. Whatever it is, his lack of experience is dangerous. He won't intend to kill you, but that doesn't mean it won't happen. You need to be extra careful."

Max tried to fit this new information into his view of the situation. No better than a square peg in a round hole. "I'm running out of time. I have no idea how long Sandra can endure whatever's happening to her, and the longer it takes me to solve this case, the more opportunities I create for Mr. Amateur to try to scare me and accidentally kill me."

"That's about right. But from everything you told me this morning, we have a clearer idea of what's going on with Holly Claypool. Perhaps if we talk with Kathy Johnson—"

"She's dead. About a year after Wade murdered Holly, Kathy took her own life. She couldn't handle the loss of her son. But, you've been to the Other a handful of times on this case and you've yet to come across her."

"I wasn't searching for her specifically. I mean, I wouldn't get my hopes up. My team of informants are quite thorough. Chances are, Kathy has moved on. Especially because when she died, she would've been looking for Wade. She wouldn't find him in the Other, so it makes sense she would move on and look there."

"Unless your informants are lying again."

"It's possible, but I'm good at reading them."

"Then what we really need is a person who can do what Sandra does, somebody who can contact Holly Claypool."

Drummond flicked the brim of his hat and grinned. "She's not going to want to help us."

"We're not going to give her a choice."

Max popped to his feet, grabbed his coat, and headed to the front door. PB and J had fallen asleep on the floor near Sandra. Mrs. Porter raised a questioning eyebrow at Max.

"I'm going out. There's coffee in the kitchen to wake you up. When I get back, I'll have a woman with me who will be able to help us. She's a specialist."

Mrs. Porter nodded with relief. "It's about time you listened to me and got a doctor. And a specialist is even better."

Getting in the car, Max wondered what his mother would say if she knew that Irene Beck was not even close to what she imagined. However, he crossed his fingers that the psychic would be exactly what he imagined.

Chapter 23

BEFORE LEAVING HIS HOUSING DEVELOPMENT, Max pulled over to the side of the road. The evening's drizzle had grown into a steady rain, and he did not want to risk an accident by driving and making a call at the same time. Irene Beck answered on the first ring.

"We made contact with Holly Claypool, and it's done something to my wife. I need your help."

"Mr. Porter, you should not have called me. I don't want to have anything to do with you people."

"Please, if I could meet with you for just a few minutes. I have only a couple of questions."

"I'm sorry, but no."

"You can't seriously tell me that you're willing to let her suffer, maybe even die."

"For crying out loud, I'm trying to get my groceries at Whole Foods and you want to lay that kind of guilt on me. It is not my responsibility if you or your wife wants to engage in such risky behavior. You play with fire, you get burned."

Max wanted to say more, but Irene had canceled the call. The steady thump of the windshield wipers echoed in his head. It created the regular beat of a killer slowly coming down a hall — *ka-clump, ka-clump*. He had never heard wipers in quite that way, and he wondered if lack of sleep and an excess of caffeine might be negatively affecting him.

Drummond said, "I'm guessing that your sudden silence means she won't be helping us."

The ghost voice snapped Max's attention back. "We're not giving up on her yet. She said she was at Whole Foods, and there's only one Whole Foods in Winston-Salem."

Max pulled back into the street and headed for Stratford

Road. Between the incessant rain and the groggy, morning drivers, traffic crawled. Max took the time to share his idea regarding how Holly Claypool's murder had played out.

"It's possible," Drummond said when Max had finished. "But I don't see why Wade would agree to any of it, or for that matter, why Holly would think summoning Jonathan Lewis could actually help."

"I figure a couple young kids in the early-70s might have some stupid ideas."

"The part about Kathy Johnson coming in on them — that carries a lot more weight. It also strengthens her motivation for taking her own life shortly after."

The grocery store had a narrow and poorly designed parking lot. The rainstorm only caused more difficulty, but after three circles around the lot, Max found an open space. Hunched over against the rain as if exiting a whirring helicopter, Max made his way into the store.

Drummond had moved ahead, and upon seeing Max, he called out, "She's over near the deli counter."

Max rapidly walked by the cash registers and straight to the deli. He saw Irene standing before a display of pies.

"You don't have time to help save my wife, but you can debate between blueberry and cherry."

Irene stepped back and her mouth dropped open. Max thought she might turn and run, but instead she shot a defiant grimace at him. "I'll give you one chance to leave. Otherwise, I'll scream for the police."

"Look at me." He put out his arms to let his drenched clothing drip onto the floor. "Do you think I would be here if I wasn't desperate? Please. All I ask is for some information."

"I don't want to be involved with you or any of this."

Despite her objection, Max noticed she had not called the police. "When we made contact with Holly, she broke free of the circle and blasted herself at Sandra. Since that moment, Sandra's been in an unconscious state. She's got a fever and I'm afraid she might never come back."

"Maybe she should go to the hospital."

Drummond flew in and let his finger draw a line across Irene's forehead. She shivered. Curling her lip, she said, "Are you threatening me?"

"Not at all," Max said, throwing a look towards Drummond. "I'm not asking you to cure her or anything like that. I'm not even asking you to take a look at her. But I don't know what's wrong with her. I don't know where to begin."

Seeing a simple way out, Irene's attitude softened. "Oh, that's all? That's easy. Your wife was attacked by a torn ghost — you know that much. If the stories are to be believed, when a torn ghost is made aware of the real world, it seeks to stay there. When you brought Holly Claypool back to our world, once she saw it, she did not want to go back to the terrible loop of sadness that she had been suffering through. So she launched herself at your wife and attached herself to your wife's soul. Or spirit or essence or whatever you believe in. Probably sensed your wife's psychic strength and was drawn to that instead of you. That's why Holly attacked me the one time I visited the firehouse. The worst part is that it doesn't work. By attaching to a person, the torn ghost returns to the loop but with a stronger sensation of the event. It becomes more real since the vessel — your wife — also feels it."

"Sandra's in the loop, too?"

"No. But she can feel it all. All of Holly's murder. Over and over."

"Is there a way to fix this? Can we stop Holly?"

"No," she said, but her eyes did not meet Max. Not even half-way. She tapped her nails against the blueberry pie container, her interest in pie-related decisions far exceeding the normal need.

"Sheesh," Drummond said. "Do I need to point out that she's lying?"

Max made a subtle shake of the head. While he guessed that talking to a ghost would not bother Irene — probably wouldn't faze her at all — the numerous people pushing their rattling carts from one food item to another might have a different outlook. He bore his gaze down on her, and she fretted under his attention.

"I've answered your questions," she said, clipping her words. "I have a life to live and would rather not waste more of my day standing here with you."

"Whatever I have to do, it doesn't scare me. I mean, it probably does, but I'll do it."

"I already told you —"

"Don't insult me."

She picked up both pies and placed them in her cart. "You have a nice day, Mr. Porter."

"Tell me, damnit!" Several passersby startled at his outburst. Lowering his voice, he added, "You don't have to be any part of it. Just point me in the right direction. Can you do that much?"

She stared at her food, twisting her lips while her fingers kneaded the cart's metal bar. She did not move.

Drummond pointed at her. "Oh, that's what this is — she can't give you the answer because she *is* the answer."

"I can't do it, huh?" Max said, and Irene nodded.

"You need somebody like me. A real psychic. And you won't be able to figure out the real psychics from the frauds until it's too late. And before you ask, I won't give you any names of authentic psychics. It would be immoral of me to send any of them into the line of fire like that."

She peeked up at Max. He thought it a strange look, one that seemed to be asking a question, but he missed the meaning. Drummond, however, caught on enough to roll a bemused laugh.

"Appeal to her greed. She's willing to do the job, but she won't do it for free."

Max said, "I can pay you. How much do you want?"

"Nothing. Really," she said, daring to act insulted.

With his mentor tone, Drummond said, "You can't be blatant about it. She's got pride. Plus, she might not even realize she wants something. Right now, she's thinking she wants to leave, but she hasn't left yet, so part of her is hungry for something. Money ain't it. Try fame."

"I know this is risky," Max said, taking a step back so as not to crowd her. "Of course, as with everything in life, the greater the risk, the bigger the reward. I mean, if you save Sandra, you'll be the woman who actually dealt with a torn ghost. Witches and psychics and healers and you name it will all want to hear from you. Book deals, private lectures — all of that would come your way. Plus, the regular customers would be pounding down your door. Heck, you might even catch the eye of one of the daytime talk shows. Maybe Oprah will want you on her television channel."

Drummond circled his hat in the air. "That's thick enough. Don't lay on anymore."

Reaching over, Irene grabbed one more pie — strawberry — and set it atop the others. "Madame Bernice."

"Who's that?" Max asked.

"That is the witch you will visit. You will see her and negotiate on my behalf so that she leaves me alone. I ... may have made a deal with her."

"You want me to break a deal with a witch for you?"

"You said you would do anything, and that's my price."

Max glanced at Drummond. The ghost shook his head but also thrust out his arms as if to say *Carry on.*

"Where do I find Madame Bernice?"

Irene eagerly wrote down the address on the back of a receipt.

As Max took the paper, he swallowed down his disgust. "You ought to learn magic. You bargain like a witch."

Chapter 24

USING THE MAP ON HIS PHONE, Max and Drummond drove into downtown High Point. Off Main Street, on Westwood, they went by the YWCA. Across the street operated a sandwich shop and behind that, a series of alleys cutting between several buildings. According to Irene, they would find Madame Bernice's store selling items of the occult back there.

Reaching to the backseat, Max grabbed an umbrella. The rain continued to pepper the ground and showed little sign of letting up. As he unlocked the door, a dark figure emerged from the alleyway — a figure the same shape as the one he had chased through the woods.

"Is that really him?"

Drummond lifted the collar of his coat as if the rain would actually hit him. "You go see Madame Bernice. I've got him this time."

With eerie quiet, Drummond glided through the front of the car, through a green dumpster, and through the hard rain. As the figure disappeared around the corner, Drummond followed.

Max waited a few minutes in case the rain might ease — North Carolina weather could be fickle. But the constant beat on the roof drowned those hopes. Popping open the umbrella as he stepped out, he checked around once to make sure no other shadowy figures planned to jump out at him. He locked the car door and made his way down to the alley.

Wet trash peppered the air with a foul fragrance in the narrow chute. A door with green- and blue-chipped paint stood on the right side as if it had no business being there. Max entered. He half-expected to hear the jingle of a bell attached at the top of the entranceway. Instead, he was met with silence.

He knew instantly that he had found the right place. Not only because of the nature of the items he saw — familiar books on the occult, jars filled with odd and revolting ingredients, every color and size candle imaginable — but also because of the number of items. Witches, Max had discovered, tended to be hoarders. From floor to ceiling, Madame Bernice's store had been filled with boxes upon boxes of junk — stacks of old newspapers, cartons of expired crackers and chips, disturbing stuffed animals, and even dusty cases of soda. While much of what he saw clearly was inadequate, only a witch with true knowledge of the craft would be able to find the useful items from the tourist trash.

Max wondered if this was where Sandra and the Sandwich Boys had gone the other day, but he quickly dismissed the thought. She specifically had avoided witches. Clearly the woman Sandra had visited knew all about such things, though.

At the far end of the store, a glass counter stretched from wall to wall. An old cash register from the 1980s took up one side of the counter while a cardboard display for cigars cluttered the other side. A door behind the counter opened and in walked a young woman dressed in a low-cut black blouse, auburn hair to her shoulders, and an inviting smile that promised far more than it would ever deliver. When she spotted Max, her practiced image faltered.

"You?" she said.

Max checked behind him, but he was the sole customer. "Have we met before?"

"You helped my ... kind enough times that word gets around. I don't think there's a witch in all of North Carolina that's not heard of Max Porter and the Porter Agency."

"I had no idea."

"Oh yes," she said, approaching the counter with a slight return of her faux-smile. "At least in my world, I'd say you're a bit famous."

"My mother would be so proud." Max watched Madame Bernice carefully, calling upon the skills Drummond had taught him. He thought her initial reaction to be odd, and he knew she had meant to say something else originally. Turning in a circle, he swept the store with his eyes, but nothing stood out.

Interrupting his thoughts, she said, "Did you come to my store simply to stand there and look around, or is there something I can help you with?"

"Irene Beck."

"I see. She's gotten desperate if she's out hiring people to do her dirty work."

Max approached the counter and splayed his fingers on the glass. "Let me be clear. I have had a horrible couple of days. Don't make it worse. I need you to back off Irene. Whatever you're holding over her, let it go."

Leaning forward on the counter, purposefully exhibiting her cleavage, she said, "You know better than that, Mr. Porter. Deals with witches have a certain way of being done."

"You can rein in your chest. I'm not interested. As for making a deal with you, what do you want?" He had no intention of cutting a deal with Madame Bernice, but he wanted to hear her response. Plus, it gave him more time to observe.

Madame Bernice backed up and readjusted her blouse. She did not look insulted but rather concerned. She had stumbled at the beginning, almost divulging some connection to him she'd rather he not know, and then attempted to distract with sex appeal. Failing that, she stood with her arms held awkwardly at her sides.

"Irene owes me so much," she said, attempting to fill her words with threat but betrayed by the tremor in her voice. "I suppose, I could be persuaded to let the matter between us go as a favor to such a notable person as yourself."

"No. I will not be owing you anything."

"In that case, I want shavings of Irene Beck's skin. At least a teaspoon. The important part is that she must give this to me fully and knowingly. You can't sneak this from her or take it without her consent."

Between the narrow aisles of moldy paper and the endless towers of scented candles, Max had missed the underlying odor — an unexpected combination of burning matches and plastic.

No, not plastic. Could it really be skin?

It didn't matter. No way would Irene accept those terms, and Max would not waste the time negotiating. Breathing only through his mouth to avoid smelling anything else, his eyes fell on a stack of papers piled on the floor next to the counter. He walked closer to it, and Madame Bernice paralleled his movement.

"Am I to take your silence as a *no?*" she said.

With a casual motion, he snatched a glimpse of the papers. Order forms. Nothing special. Except clearly special to Madame Bernice. As he brought his head up, unsure of what to say next, he saw the name at the top of the order form — Bernice Mobley.

Triumph altered his posture. She saw the change, too. She backed towards the door.

"Don't run off," he said. "If you leave, I'll have to go talk to the Mobley Coven in order to figure this all out."

Like a nervous actress on her first audition, Madame Bernice bit her lip as she rocked from foot to foot. "What exactly, that is, I mean did Irene truly send you or are you here for Lena?"

Lena Mobley ran the coven for the matriarch, Grandma Mobley. Max understood entirely too well why Madame Bernice would be worried. Lena was downright scary.

"I'm here for Irene. But if you won't help me, I might have to talk with Lena."

Max had made a mistake. He knew it the moment he had finished speaking. He didn't know exactly where he went wrong, but Madame Bernice's fears slipped away as her smile grew. She sauntered to the counter with the confidence of a trained seductress. "Well then, we might still be able to make a deal."

"I'm not getting you skin."

"Relax," she said, dripping amusement and fear. "All I need from you is silence. That case you worked on for the coven — dear me, that sent shockwaves through the witch community. The tension between the Mobley Coven and the Magi keeps getting worse. Trouble is brewing and I want none of it."

"Is that what this store is all about? You're trying to build a rainy day fund?"

"Bless your heart, you are really not grasping the enormity of what's going on. There's a war coming. Witch against witch. People are going to die, and they'll probably be the lucky ones. Have you ever seen two witches fight? Did any of your research ever show you what a witch war can do to a town? Or a city? Hell, if I were you I wouldn't even feel safe hanging around the entire state."

There it was. "You're running. This isn't rainy day money or even emergency money. You're selling off everything you can, whatever you have to, so you can get as far away from here as possible."

"You should do the same."

"Too many people around here I love."

She rolled her eyes, betraying her youth. "When I joined the coven, I thought I had become part of the greatest sisterhood in existence. These weren't just sorority sisters, these women went beyond the notion of family. We belong to each other with a depth that you could never grasp. It's like our souls are entwined."

"Yet you're abandoning them."

"I never signed up for war. I have spent the last two years trying to talk them down from this ledge, but Lena wants to jump. And the rest of them are going to follow. Not me."

"As long as I keep my mouth shut."

"You will. I promise to release Irene Beck from what she owes me. In exchange, you will never give me up to Lena or any of the coven. That's the deal. In case you are too stupid to recognize this, I'll point out to you that witches never make a deal as fair as this. Consider today your one-time special offer."

At first, Max did not answer. Madame Bernice had spoken the truth — witches did not make offers like this. So, why did Madame Bernice? She had the ability to curse Max. She had no need to bargain with him. Bargaining with Witches 101 — *Never make a deal that doesn't make sense from the witch's point of view.*

In a flash, he saw the mistake he had previously made. The

change in Madame Bernice came only after Max mentioned that he had not spoken to Lena yet. That's what gave Madame Bernice confidence. But it also posed her with a problem. If she cursed Max in any form — took away his speech, removed his tongue, caused him pain should he mention certain words — the rest of the witch community would know. After all, Max and the Porter Agency had reached at least a level of basic notoriety. Cursing Max would be the same as shining a light on her activities. The Mobley Coven would know, and her dream of escaping them would die.

Turned out his mistake gave him the leverage he needed. "You have a deal," he said.

As he turned to go, she said, "To be clear, while I am still here in North Carolina, it is best that I never see you again. If I do, I will consider that a breach of our agreement."

Max flashed a big smile. "Wouldn't have it any other way."

Returning to his car, he jumped over several large puddles. The biggest one, however, had formed underneath his car door. Opening the car while on tiptoes, he felt glad nobody was around to see him. Once he sat, pulled in his umbrella, and close the door, he looked over to find Drummond staring back.

"Why can't you just walk through a puddle?"

"Says the ghost who floats over them all." Max turned on the car and blasted the heat. "I got things squared away for Irene. What happened with you? Who is this guy following me?"

All the smarmy sarcasm on Drummond's face vanished. Max had the sudden urge to provoke his partner into furthering the repartee — anything to avoid the information that tied to Drummond's dark look. But Drummond was clearly not ready to be witty.

"The short of it is that I followed the guy about a block west. He had his car parked on a side street. When I moved in close, I planned to hop a ride in the backseat, that's when I learned that our friend carried with him a ghost ward. Blasted me all the way back to the YWCA. I'm guessing your new witch friend supplied him with it. By the time I got back, his car was gone."

"Why such a look? You had me scared."

"I don't think you have to be scared, but caution would be advisable. The fact that this guy had a ghost ward says he knows about me."

"So? This isn't the first person we've ever dealt with like that."

"Yeah, but who in our current case would have that knowledge?"

"Oh."

"Exactly. Oh. Either Peter Rathburn is secretly full of occult knowledge, or —"

"Or this whole thing with the Magi and the Mobley Coven is hotter than I realized. Okay, no matter what is going on with all of these witches, we still have a case to solve and my wife to save. The witch I just dealt with makes me think that any problems Mother Hope is stirring up won't be causing us trouble right now."

"Other than this guy going around taking shots at you."

"He hasn't hit me yet."

"Very funny. I'd like my living partners to stay living."

Max pulled out his phone. "Me, too. So let's help Sandra." He called up Irene, told her he had fixed her situation, and that she should meet him at his house. He then texted her the address.

Driving back, he filled in Drummond on the brewing witch war. Twenty minutes later he pulled into his development. He should've known better than to feel optimistic. Up ahead, fire engines flashing red lights and neighbors gawking clogged the street. And Max's house — burning to the ground.

Chapter 25

PLUMES OF BLACK SMOKE darkened the gray overcast sky. Flashes of orange sprang through the smoke like destructive fireflies. Max launched from the car.

Running towards the building, he tried to call out to Sandra but only managed a garbled cry. As he broke through the crowd and dashed by one of the engines, two large men formed a wall in front of him — Peter Rathburn and Captain Renner. Drummond raced ahead into the inferno.

"It's okay," Peter said, his arm holding Max in place like concrete. "Don't worry. Nobody's in the house. We've had guys search it top to bottom. She's not in there."

Max heard the words but his brain refused to process them. Peter kept repeating himself. An eternal minute later, Drummond slid through the blazing front door. Shaken but relieved, he nodded. "She's not in there. None of them are. The house is empty."

Max's knees buckled, and Captain Renner caught him. Easing Max to the back ledge of a fire engine, Renner said, "It's going to be okay."

Watching firefighters move with coordinated urgency, Max's body went numb. His wife, his mother, the Sandwich Boys — all were safe. His home, however, looked like an enormous campfire, and the flames mesmerized as they always do. The dense crackling played along with the rich aroma of burning wood. Only the occasional crash of glass or collapse of a wall broke the serene illusion.

His life floated into the hot air, reduced to smoke and ash. The fine desk in his study, their treasured books kept in the bedroom, all of Sandra's research on witchcraft and the occult — gone. Their favorite clothes, his reading chair, the comfort of breakfast at the kitchen table — gone. Photo albums, school yearbooks, the couch they would cuddle on while watching television — all gone.

Anguished tears hovered behind his eyes. Oddest of all — he shivered. Intense waves of heat hit him like a high tide of fire, yet he shivered.

"How did this happen?" Max said to nobody in particular.

Peter observed the work of his peers. "We won't be able to answer that until a fire inspector can get onto the premises. At the earliest, that won't be until tomorrow. Once they get this fire under control and then out, it'll still take a while before it's safe to pick around in there."

At least, it's raining, Max thought. Except as the thought hit him, he noticed that the rain had stopped. Of course, it did.

He did not think that witchcraft could control the weather, but he didn't know for sure. He clenched his fists. If he found out that Mother Hope had done this to him, no curse or ward would protect her.

Max closed his eyes, but the image of his home aflame echoed behind his eyelids. He turned away. With his eyes on the ground, he only saw shoes and boots. In particular, he noticed Peter Rathburn and Captain Renner wore sneakers. Letting his gaze lift, he found that they were not dressed in firefighter gear at all.

"What are you two doing here? I can't imagine this part of town is covered by your station. That's got to be too far away."

Peter said, "You're right. We're off-duty. The captain and I were having lunch up the road when we heard the call. I recognized the address, so we came to offer our help, if needed."

"You were going to help dressed like that?"

"I'm trying to save my job." He muddled a weak laugh. "We came to help you and Sandra. The men and women taking care of your house can do the job easily. I had tried calling Sandra, but there was no answer." Lowering his head toward Max while keeping an eye on Captain Renner, Peter whispered, "And after last night, I was worried about her."

"She's fine," Max said. Trying to take the bite out of his terse reply, he added, "Thanks for coming out. I appreciate it."

Back on his feet, Max headed to his car. He would have to call the insurance agent, probably would need some paperwork from the fire department, and should notify their realtor to take the house off the market. Before any of that, however, he had to speak with his mother.

When he looked at his phone, he found several texts from J. Together, they read: *Grandma saw somebody snooping *her word*Got nervous We left Went to her apt.*

"Where you going?" Peter asked, taking several steps towards Max.

"Nothing I can do here," Max said over his shoulder.

"You can't leave."

Max halted. "I'm going to see my wife and tell her that everything we own is gone. You have a problem with that?" He turned his head and glowered at Peter like a lone wolf raring for a fight.

"No, no. Of course not. Sandra should know. Just tell me where you're going, so I can reach you once things are done here."

"You got our cell numbers. Call us."

Max trudged towards his car. Drummond appeared by his side as he drove off. He stopped a block away and pulled out his phone. His first call went to his mother. She confirmed J's message, although she used many more words. After promising that he was on his way, and leaving out the current condition of the house, he ended the call. Next, he called Irene Beck. He told her there had been a change in plans and gave her the address for his mother's apartment. As Irene asked what the problem was, he ended the call. Back on Silas Creek Parkway, Max could not release his clenched muscles.

"Tough break," Drummond said. "I don't know if you can think clearly, but remember your family is safe. That's all that really matters. The rest is junk."

"I know. But they're only safe for the moment. When we were at Madame Bernice's, we saw the man who has been attacking me. You followed him. That was in High Point. There is no way he could have gotten all the way to Winston-Salem, reached our house, stalked the place enough to have been noticed by my mother, waited for them to leave, then snuck in and set up some incendiary device. It's just not possible."

"He had to have help."

"I was sort of hoping you'd have a different conclusion."

Drummond gestured behind with his thumb. "You think it's Peter?"

"You mean, the guy who has no business being anywhere near my house and just happens to be having a drink nearby? The same guy with all the knowledge required to burn down the house effectively, efficiently, and probably without leaving any significant trace of arson? The same guy who is right now standing by that house waiting for a chance to remove any evidence from the scene? Yeah, I think it's him. Don't you?"

"Absolutely. I'm just glad you're finally saying it, too."

Without another word, they drove the rest of the way to Mrs. Porter's apartment.

Chapter 26

BEFORE THE APARTMENT DOOR HAD EVEN CLOSED, Mrs. Porter clutched her son's chin. "What's wrong? You look awful."

With that simple question, all of Max's bravado drained away. He pulled her hand down, and his shaking fingers stopped her from speaking again. Feeling tears escape his eyes, he wrapped his arms around his mother.

"It's all gone."

His head rested on her shoulder as she patted his back. Through blurry eyes, he saw PB and J standing several feet away. They watched him and awkwardly waited.

"Don't mean to be rude," Drummond said, floating half in/half out the front door, "but can we move this fully inside?"

Keeping his arm around his mother, Max shuffled into the main room and flopped on the couch. He sniffled and dabbed at his tears. As Drummond flew in, the boys closed around Max.

"What happened?" PB finally braved.

Reaching out to put a hand on either boys' shoulder, Max said, "There's been a fire." He went on to explain about the destruction of their home. By the time he finished, PB and J blubbered at the loss. They didn't own much, and little of what possessions they had were at the house, yet they took it hard — perhaps they feared a financial hit might cause complications for their own futures.

Max thought he should say something, assure them that all would be fine, but seeing the uncertainty in their eyes only deepened his own sadness. He opened his mouth and his throat tightened. He clenched his fists and fought back the urge to wail.

Mrs. Porter stomped into her kitchen and returned with two paper towels. Handing them to the boys, she said, "Enough with all this crying. You'd think something important happened. Yes, yes, I know. A fire is a terrible thing. But nobody was hurt, nobody was killed. Boys, of all the people I've ever known, the two of you should understand how meaningless possessions are. They come and go." She perched on the edge of the couch, creating a tight circle amongst them. "It's family that matters. Not how many things you have or how nice of a house you live in. Not how much money you have or how many people know your name. All that matters is having your family safe. Because in the end, only your family will ever have your back. Right now, the danger to this family is not some fire that's burning down Max's house. That's unfortunate, but it can be handled easily enough. The real threat is happening to Sandra. It's up to us to help her. She's our family. She's all that matters now."

Max and the boys stared at Mrs. Porter as if she had popped out of a book wearing a rainbow-striped leotard.

Mrs. Porter sat taller. "What? Just because that woman shows me very little respect doesn't mean she's not family."

Fearing his mother might get on a ranting roll, Max sprang to his feet and cleared his throat. "You're right. We need to focus on Sandra."

J leapt over to Mrs. Porter's bedroom door. "She's in here."

Painted baby blue and decked out with an overwhelming number of photographs depicting Max at every age, the bedroom smelled of Mrs. Porter's unique personal blend — floral perfume and medicinal mint. Despite the familiarity, Max found the room to be a heavy weight as if the walls had expectations. He had plenty of his own at the moment and none concerned his ambitions or future prospects. Between the razing of his home and the direct words of his mother, Max's life focused down to a pinpoint of clarity.

Only one thing mattered — Sandra.

He stood at the foot of the bed and watched over his wife like a General strategizing over a war map. A battle raged under the quiet of her paling skin, and he had to find some way to send reinforcements.

He felt the spectral cold of his partner approaching. With his Fedora held against his chest, Drummond spoke with uncommon sensitivity. "I wish I could tell you that everything would be okay, that Sandra was fine, and that the cure for her would be easy. You're too smart for that kind of nonsense. But I can promise you this — she's a fighter and so am I. The three of us have taken on some powerful and deadly people, and we've won. So, you have my word. I will not give up. Don't you give up, either."

"Wasn't even considering it."

"I know. I'm not worried about this moment."

Max heard his mother answering the front door as he looked at Drummond. "Do you know something you're not telling me?"

"Only what I've learned over my long existence. When you deal with ghosts and witches and all of the kinds of things we deal with, there comes a point where you wonder if it's not better to end somebody's life than let them continue on suffering under the pressure of some curse. I'm telling you, as one who has spent decades under a curse, as long as you continue to believe in your wife, support her, be there for her, then no curse she suffers is too great."

"I appreciate what you're trying to say, but you don't have to worry about me. You forget I'm suffering under a curse, too. I may not talk about it often, but I'm always aware of it."

Mrs. Porter entered her bedroom with Irene Beck following close behind. The Sandwich Boys watched from the hall.

Offering no more than a quick nod to Max, Irene stepped over to Sandra's side. As she looked over his slumbering wife, cold dread filled Max's heart. Sandra looked more like a corpse than a patient. Irene wafted the air above Sandra and sniffed sharply. She then inspected Sandra's hand, prodding it with her thumbs and rolling her fingers along the back before setting the hand gently on the bed.

When she turned her attention to Max, she dried her sweaty

hands on her legs. "I'll need a focal object. Something of Sandra's that is valuable to her. Not financially valuable, but emotionally valuable. And if it also happens to be an object that she has used before in one of your cases, something that might have a psychic relationship to her, that's even better."

Max staggered back, gut-punched by this simple request. "Please tell me you can do this without an object."

Frowning, Irene said, "Not really. I mean, I suppose I could try, but it would be far more dangerous to me and to Sandra. Might not even work."

When Max did not respond, Mrs. Porter said, "Their house burned down. The poor things. We don't have an object dear to Sandra anymore."

Irene looked ill which turned Max's stomach worse than it already had felt. Lacing her fingers in front of her, she said, "I'm sorry. I don't think this will work."

Never taking his eyes off his wife, Max said, "Can the object be living?"

"Yes," Irene said. "But I can't do this with you. A spouse has too much history, too much energy. All those years of fights and makeups, those special romantic evenings and the heavy disappointments — it all becomes too muddled. Instead of becoming a focal point, you would be like spilling a gallon of paint on a canvas. You would simply wash over everything. I need something that will help me see the canvas not destroy it."

"What about the boys? She loves them, but we haven't known them that long. We don't have years of history with them. They've also worked on cases with us. They might have some kind of psychic relationship because of that."

As Irene thought through the possibility, Mrs. Porter waved the boys in. Giving J a hug and then PB, she said, "I know you two were listening. How could you not? So, what do you say?"

"Tell us what we've got to do," J said.

PB nodded. "Yeah, we'll do anything for her."

Irene wiped at the corners of her eyes. "Sandra is very lucky to have you boys. Okay, we can make this work."

As she seated the boys on the bed, opposite her and with

Sandra between, Max struggled to keep from bursting into tears. The walls threatened to crumble upon him, bury him in the debris of all he had lost and all that might still be taken from him. Yet here these two boys sat, willfully risking their safety for the woman he loved.

"What do we do now?" PB asked.

Regaining her composure, Irene said, "It's simple but important. All you have to do is sit very still and concentrate on Sandra. Think of a happy memory involving her. You don't have to think of the same memory, so pick something specific to you. Don't touch her. Don't touch me. Don't even touch each other. You can close your eyes or keep them open, that's up to you, but this is all about what's going on in your head. Think of that happy memory, picture it as clearly as you can, make it so you can see it, smell it, taste it. Everything. And last, don't make a sound."

J laughed. "This is going to be easy."

"I know you think that, but you're wrong. It's very hard to quiet your mind. It's very hard to be still. Our brains like to play games with us, and the moment your brain realizes what you're trying to do, it'll start messing with you. You feel fine right now, but once we get going, I guarantee that your brain will find itches that need to be scratched. You'll start thinking about Sandra and some happy memory, and then your brain will send in the monkeys of thought. They'll start jumping around, distracting you, making you forget what you're supposed to be doing. If that happens — when that happens — don't feel bad, and don't freak out. Take a deep breath, close your eyes, and start focusing again on that happy memory. This is hard stuff. It's kind of like a very specialized meditation. Buddhist monks and people who study yoga or tai chi — all of those kinds of people work hard at meditation and they never perfect it. The key thing is to keep trying."

The boys straightened their backs as they donned their most serious looks. When Irene turned her attention toward Sandra, both boys peeked at Max. In that brief moment, he fought back the urge to laugh. The boys wanted to help, and they would do what was asked of them, but they clearly thought the brain monkeys had come for Irene a while ago and never returned.

From her shoulder bag, Irene pulled out an incense stick and a stand. She set it up on the bedside table and lit the stick. Max could feel his mother stiffen, but she kept silent. She would probably want the place fumigated afterwards.

Irene then tapped away on her cell phone. A second later, the steady hum of Tibetan singing bowls filled the room — gentle and unending. She raised her arms and let them hover over Sandra's body.

"Okay, boys. Take a deep breath and concentrate. Remember — no sounds, no touching. Just focus on a happy memory with Sandra."

Taking a deep breath of her own, Irene closed her eyes. Max and his mother became a riveted audience, motionless and quiet, afraid to miss a single detail. Even Drummond did not speak.

"Holly Claypool. Can you hear me?" Irene waited for a response. When none came, she readjusted her hands in the air. With her fingers dancing as if playing the piano to a somber song, she said, "Holly Claypool. Let go of this woman. It's time for you to move on." Again, no response.

Looking like a child ready to give up because learning something new was hard, she offered a pitiful pout toward Max. When she opened her mouth, however, her fingers stopped moving and her eyes popped wide. Tight gurgling creaked out of her throat. Her muscles constricted as she stood like a petrified tree.

Max reached up but remembered Irene's instructions to the boys. He didn't know if touching her, trying to help her, could hurt Sandra. He lowered his hand.

He swore her lifeless face begged for help. But as she continued to stare at him, the color of her eyes altered. It darkened. Her jaw slowly opened and closed. And as it loosened, so did Irene's throat. She could speak. But the voice Max heard did not belong to Irene Beck. He had heard the voice before, though — heard it during the middle of the night in a firehouse kitchen.

"You?" Holly Claypool said. "What are you doing here?"

As Max debated whether or not to answer, Irene's arm slapped downward and her head whipped to face Sandra. She stiffened more, and Max worried the strain on her muscles might cause permanent damage. Letting out another strangled sound, she collapsed. When she hit the floor, the Sandwich Boys flew backwards into the wall as if yanked by unseen ropes.

Max lunged across the room towards PB and J. Pointing at Irene, he commanded his mother, "Check on her."

PB raised his hands as if the police had arrived. "I didn't say a word. I didn't touch nothing."

"You're fine. You didn't do anything wrong." Max stepped over the boy to get a better look at J. "Hey there. You okay?"

J's head lolled as his eyes struggled to focus. Licking the inside of his mouth, J rested his hand on top of his head. "Won't stop spinning."

"Let's be glad that's the worst of it."

"I don't know. I might throw up."

On the other side of the bed, Mrs. Porter helped Irene to her feet. Though the psychic looked shaken, she appeared uninjured. Without a word, she grabbed her bag. While she snuffed out her incense and packed her belongings, Drummond floated over the bed.

"Sandra's still here," he said. "But I think we're losing her. She seems dimmer."

Max hurried over to Irene. "Why are you packing up?"

"I tried," she said. "You saw what happened. Even if I wanted to try that again, and I don't, there is no way I will take a chance with those boys' lives. My advice to you — take your wife to the hospital. Treat her like a coma patient. At least that way, they'll be able to stabilize her, keep her going, and if you're lucky, Holly Claypool will eventually leave on her own."

"You can't do this. You're abandoning her."

"I didn't want to have anything to do with this in the first place. I warned you to leave Holly Claypool alone. You have nobody to blame but yourself."

Irene turned to leave, but Mrs. Porter stood in her way — hands on hips and a deep scowl that would cause an Army Ranger to hesitate. "You are not going anywhere."

Clutching her bag, Irene said, "You can't keep me here. I have rights."

"Lady, I am not the government."

"I don't know what you think I can do. I've tried. I failed. Going through the motions again is not going to get Holly Claypool to talk. She's made it clear that she has no interest in dealing with me."

"What about acting as a psychic link for Max?"

Getting hit in the head with a baseball bat could not have stunned Max as much as his mother's words. "What did you just say?"

With a shrug, Mrs. Porter said, "It's no big deal. For a short time, long before you were born, I had an interest in psychics. I read about them, I went to see fortunetellers, all of that stuff. But eventually I realized that I did not have the gift. So, I let it all go."

Drummond said, "I cannot believe I heard that."

Max looked around the room in disbelief. Seeing PB help J stand convinced him that he wasn't hallucinating everything. "How is this possible? You've always acted disdainful of the very idea of ghosts and spells."

"Well, that stuff is ridiculous. Real psychics are another matter. Besides, ever since you moved down here, all I started hearing from you was strange bits and pieces. Once I got here and saw what was going on, it was clear to me that part of you had the same interest I once had. Unfortunately, you fell for the charlatan side of things. Witches? Really? I didn't want to see you get hurt like I did. I suppose the way you kids talk about it now would be to say that I fell into a bit of depression. It took a while, but I walked away from all of that and focused on building my family. I was afraid that if I showed you the real world of psychics, it would spark your interest. Trust me, dear, if I don't have the gift, then you don't have it, either."

Irene said, "I do have the gift, and I'm telling you that what you're asking of me won't work. I will not link with Max."

Max rubbed his head. "Hold on. I'm still trying to catch up with the idea that my mother accepts the concept of psychics. The idea that she wanted to be one is something that has to be dealt with another day."

"Don't be so dramatic," Mrs. Porter said. "I know you idolize me as this perfect mother, but I was young once. We all go through stages of experimenting with different ideas. It's not that big of a deal."

Snorting a laugh, Drummond said, "Your mother is a real kick in the pants."

Speaking slowly while he thought, Max said, "Let's just put aside your history and focus on your idea. How does this linking work?"

Mrs. Porter raised an eyebrow at Irene, but when the psychic refused to speak, Max's mother said, "It's pretty much what it sounds like. Right now, Irene is the only one in this room who can communicate with Holly Claypool. If she's willing, Irene can act like a phone line between you and Holly's spirit."

"It's too dangerous," Irene said. "This isn't like me simply trying to talk with Holly. This would be connecting you directly with her energy. And since her energy is locked in a loop of her final, most likely horrible memories, then you'll be locked in there with her. It's very risky to the psychic doing the linking."

"Sounds pretty risky for me, too," Max said. PB and J still wobbled on their feet and they had not been anywhere close to being linked with Holly. If Max went along with this and Holly rejected them, she may throw him through the wall. Might even snap his neck. "I don't like this."

"That's smart. I don't like it either."

"Too bad were going to do it."

Irene attempted stepping around Mrs. Porter, but Mrs. Porter continued to block her way. Holding back tears but unable to control the mousey fear in her voice, Irene said, "You can't keep me prisoner."

Mrs. Porter said, "You whine a lot. What kind of mother did

you have? I would never let Max act the way you do."

"If you think insulting me and my mother is going to get me to help you, you're crazy."

"Let me tell you what's crazy. Thinking that I will simply stand aside and let you walk out that door when you are the only chance we have to save that woman, now that's crazy. Thinking that my son would simply shrug and say *oh well* because you are afraid, that's crazy. Did you not hear Max? He recognizes the danger involved with this, but he's going to do it anyway. Do you want to know why? It's because I raised him right. He will do anything to protect those he loves. And if that doesn't convince you, then let me make it even clearer — there is no way in hell that I will ever let a psychic ruin my life again. Got it?"

Max didn't think he could handle being stunned anymore that day, but then Irene nodded her head and set her bag on the floor.

Chapter 27

THE NEXT TWENTY MINUTES spun circles around Max's head. Still reeling from the loss of his home and possessions, he barely had the mental room to deal with his mother's old hobby. At best, he managed to shove all of these problems into a dull, buzzing ball in the back of his head.

Irene had him stand motionless in the bedroom while she moved her hands through the air around his body. He was neither to speak nor move — a prisoner without chains. Though her hands reacted to different sections of his body, vibrating over his chest and falling limp near his feet, he felt nothing unusual. If not for his previous experiences, he might have returned to the idea that Irene was a fraud.

"When we begin," Irene said, "you may encounter some disorientation or even pain. This is normal. It's part of your psychic energy traveling through me and linking up with Holly."

Drummond floated near Sandra, his lips pursed, his finger tapping his chin. "You should know this is all new to me. I've never come across this kind of thing, so don't count on having too much time. If it all starts to look fishy, I'm going to put the freeze on Irene to break whatever link she creates."

"Once the link is established, if all goes well, you will be inside Holly Claypool's final memories. Her last moments. You can interact with her, but it will be difficult."

"Just don't get caught up in the moment. Stay focused. Remember why you're there — you've got to save Sandra's life."

Badgered by a ghost and a psychic — exactly the way Max wanted to spend his days. Though not permitted to speak, they couldn't stop him from thinking sarcastic thoughts.

Irene continued, "You must be very careful while you are in there. You can't change the past because it's only a memory. Don't try to save her or interfere no matter what happens."

"The key thing," Drummond went on, "is to pay attention to details. We know somebody interrupted Holly and Wade's attempt at witchcraft — who was it?"

"Your presence in her memory might disturb her. She might strike out at you. Be careful not to hurt her. But be more careful not to get hurt. This isn't a dream. Your physical body is linked to your psychic projection. If you die in her memory, you die for real."

"Don't be spooked with all that death talk. Stay focused. Who interrupted them and why? And if you can, try to figure out why Wade Johnson even agreed to play with witchcraft in the first place. That part bothers me."

"Speak gently with her and explain to her how she is hurting your wife. If you can get her to release your wife and speak with me, you can promise that I will help her to move on."

"Ignore the psychic. What you've got to do is solve the case. Once we understand how she became a torn ghost, then we can free her."

While Irene and Drummond ping-ponged their thoughts against Max, Mrs. Porter ordered the boys to bring up towels and cleaning supplies. "From what I remember, this can be a messy business."

Irene stepped back and appraised Max as if he were a marble statue. "I think we're ready. You can move now and talk."

Sitting on a chair that PB had provided, Irene held Sandra's hand and reached out for Max. He took her hand as she closed her eyes to concentrate. Though she said he could speak, he decided to close his eyes as well. Drummond was right — he needed to be ready for whatever was about to happen.

Chapter 28

IT STARTED WITH A LURCH FORWARD as if somebody had shoved him from behind. Irene's fingers felt cold yet heat radiated through the back of his hand and up his arm. Like a sudden drop on a rollercoaster, the world flew away from him, leaving his head spinning and his thoughts tumbling.

Memories flashed by while others fluttered across his vision — first meeting Sandra, climbing trees with his best friend, a first kiss, cheating on a spelling test in the sixth grade and getting caught, moving to North Carolina, seeing Drummond for the first time standing in the middle of his desk, fighting the Hulls and Mother Hope and the ghost of Dr. Connor at the Devil's Tramping Ground. That was in the first two seconds. The next five seconds flooded more memories in a deluge that threatened to rent the air from Max's lungs.

Then all went dark.

He heard the droning rumble of a clothes dryer. Humid air covered his skin. He smelled a strange blend of soap and sweat.

His vision irised open as if he watched an old film. He stood in a basement laundry room with gray cinderblock walls, a small tiled floor angled toward a drain, two coin-operated washing machines and two coin-operated dryers, and at the far end of the room, he saw Holly Claypool.

Irene had done it.

He stood in Holly's memory. Which explained the paisley dress she wore and the fact that the laundry only cost a quarter. It was 1973.

She paced the narrow room, squeezing the bridge of her nose as she mumbled an argument in her head. When she reached the end of the room, she stared right at Max. She turned away and paced back.

Irene had said he would be able to communicate with her, so either the psychic was wrong or Holly had not attuned to his presence yet. While he suspected the former, he didn't want to take any chances with the latter. He looked behind to find a wooden set of stairs that reached a metal landing toward the door out of the laundry room. Plenty of room underneath the staircase to hide. As he situated himself behind an old crate, he heard the door above him open.

Holly whirled around.

"Wade," she said, the name coming out filled with relief and anxiety.

Wade Johnson came down the stairs, walked straight to her, and wrapped her in his arms. As Max had seen in the photographs, Wade was a good-looking man. Even when distorted with 1970s style, the man's chiseled handsomeness broke through.

"What's going on? You sounded upset on the phone. And now we're meeting down here?" His voice creaked as if he had woken up only minutes before.

Drumming the fingers of one hand into the palm of the other, Holly resumed her pacing. "I have something to tell you. Oh, I just don't know if I should. I already spoke with your mother, but I know what I know and I don't see how we can make it if we start off with a big secret between us."

Wade stopped Holly's movement by placing his hands on her shoulders. "Baby doll, slow down. I can't follow what you're trying to say." As she gazed up at him, her whole body shaking, his eyes twinkled as a wide grin broke over his mouth. "Oh, are you telling me — are you pregnant?"

Wiping a tear from her cheek, she said, "No, but I can't even begin to tell you how wonderful it is to see that smile on your face." She held him around the neck and pulled his head down into a long embrace. Max worried they might take things a lot further — he had no interest in sitting through a memory that played out like a bad porn movie — but he reminded himself that this was her final memory. A memory already quite different from what he thought had happened, but that didn't change the outcome. Bad things loomed. As Wade's hand slipped down her side, she pushed him back. "Hold your horses. We do have to talk."

Leaning against a washing machine, Wade nodded and pulled out a joint from his shirt pocket. He lit up and inhaled deeply before offering it to Holly. After a short toke, she returned the joint. He waited, but when she did not speak, he smoked again.

Part of Max wanted to jump out and urge these two young kids to start talking with each other. It was good that they had met down here, that Holly had decided to fess up, to be open and honest, so that the foundation of their relationship would be firm. He had learned the hard way that a marriage needed that level of honesty. It was a miracle that he and Sandra had survived considering all the secrets they had kept in the past.

"I talked with your mom," Holly finally said.

Wade pinched out the cigarette and set it back in his pocket. "Yeah, you said that."

"I did. Why is this so hard?"

"Look, I love you. It's that simple. You got nothing to worry about. You can tell me anything."

"I sure hope so." Rolling back her shoulders and lifting her chin, she spoke in a flurry. "Last weekend, you and your old war buddy Joe were drinking and talking up through the night. I heard you guys out on the porch. Well, you mentioned an uncle, Uncle Billy, and he said he came from Kentucky. I don't know why, but those words got me thinking. I guess because other stuff you've said over the years or maybe something your mom said. I can't explain it. I decided that I needed to know more about your family and — I don't mean this as pressure — but it seems like we're kind of headed to get married."

Wade grinned. "I'd say we're that way."

"Exactly. So, I had to be sure."

"About what?"

"When you talked about Uncle Billy, you made it sound like he had something wrong. You told Joe about how over-the-top he was, angry all the time, stuff like that."

"Baby doll, Uncle Billy served in Korea. The guy's got shellshock."

"That's not what I heard. So I did a little digging — I went to the public records, checked some of the yearbooks, you know, library stuff."

Max cringed. Even back then people just didn't respect the value of good research.

"But I wasn't getting where I wanted to be," she said. "So I figured it'd be best to just go talk to your mom. That's what I did. I was a little worried that something might be wrong in Uncle Billy's head — not from the war but something that he was born with. Something I'd want to be aware of, ready for in case it happened to our child." Pacing again, she said, "I know I sound silly. Maybe I was. But it doesn't matter. It was these crazy thoughts that got me into your living room talking with your mom. And I must have said enough that she thought I knew more than I did. Because she told me the truth."

Wade uttered a marijuana-induced giggle. "What truth?"

She let it out. In an explosion of words that billowed one revelation after another, she hit him with the full story of his lineage. She led him back to his ancestors in Kentucky and how they traced to Jonathan Lewis. She told him of Naomi Wise's murder and Jonathan Lewis's guilt.

"This wasn't just any murder," she said, stepping closer to him, her eyes open, hoping he would forgive her for all that she had to say. "It wasn't just the brutality. It wasn't just that she was kind and sweet and innocent. I think what really upset people was the way he used them all to hide his crime. The way he lied to all those around him. People don't like to be made a fool of."

Wade turned away from her and pounded his fist on the top of the washing machine. "What does any of this have to do with us?"

"People don't forget. Not with something like this. It's one of those things that has dug deep into the family and taken hold. It's like the Hatfields and McCoys — in a way, it's become part of your identity, part of your core family identity."

"It's not part of my anything!" He kicked the dryer for good measure. "Wait — are you telling me that your family are descendants of Naomi Wise? Is that why this is a problem?"

"Naomi died before she ever had a child. She has no descendants."

"Then where is this whole Hatfields and McCoys part?"

"On one side is your family and on the other side are all the descendants of the people living in those towns at the time."

"What? In all of North Carolina?"

Softly, she said, "I think so."

"I don't accept that. It's just wrong. Why should anybody care about a murder from over a century ago? I just came back from a jungle where murder was a daily occurrence. Nobody cares about that — not unless they can use it for a little fame or to fit in with the in-crowd. But this old, old murder? Why should this matter?"

"Because," a voice said from above — a voice that sounded familiar to Max, "I won't let a family of violent sons of bitches destroy her, too."

Holly snapped her focus to the landing above the stairs. "You? What are you doing here?"

As Max lifted his head, attempting to angle his neck to see who had arrived, he felt the floor beneath him disappear. The lurch from before, the one that felt as if he had been shoved from behind, came upon him followed by the rollercoaster drop. All went dark. And as light gently returned, he found himself standing in the laundry room alone — alone with Holly as she paced in anticipation of Wade's arrival.

The loop had started again.

Max backed his way under the stairs. He tried to work a better angle with which to see the platform above. As he craned his neck one direction and another, never meeting the success he hoped for, Holly cleared her throat.

He didn't recall her doing that the previous time through the loop. Statue still, he listened. She cleared her throat again — this time in an obvious attempt for attention.

Cautiously, he turned his head. She stared straight at him.

Stepping to the side, her eyes indicated a broom closet at the far end of the room. He took a breath, ready to ask a question despite Irene's warnings, but Holly returned to her pacing as if nothing had happened.

Letting his intuition play out, Max rose from underneath the stairs and risked crossing the laundry room. As he walked by Holly, he thought she snuck a peek at him. He opened the broom closet and slipped inside. Keeping the door cracked open, he had a narrow but clear view across the room.

This time when Wade Johnson came to the door, Max witnessed the lustful smile on the man's face. Wade must have thought this meeting would lead to a romantic encounter. But one look at Holly caused Wade's expression to drop.

As the conversation between the two lovers enacted once more, Max had to shake off the guilt of a voyeur. He watched this private moment for only one reason — to save Sandra. Yet he still felt a layer of grime settling on his skin like a teenager leafing through porn magazines while keeping one ear attune in case his mother opened the door.

He watched as Wade held Holly by the shoulders, called her *Baby doll*, and broke into an enthusiastic grin. "Oh, are you telling me — are you pregnant?"

He watched as they smoked marijuana to find the strength for their talk.

He watched as Holly raced through the words about Uncle Billy, Kentucky, and how she eventually pieced together Wade's connection to the notorious Johnathan Lewis.

He watched how Wade's anger overcame him and he attacked the washing machine, how Holly tried to make him see that hatred passed down from generations did not obey logic, and how Wade refused to accept the situation.

And then Max heard the familiar voice. "Because I won't let a family of violent sons of bitches destroy her, too."

Then Holly snapped her focus to the landing. "You? What are you doing here?"

From the broom closet, Max saw a young man wearing black slacks, a short-sleeved white shirt and black tie, and a simple flattop. He looked ready to crunch numbers with a slew of accountants at an old law firm. One thing gave away his identity — the sharp break in the middle of his nose. Max had no doubt. This was Holly's brother. Floyd Claypool.

"He's a killer, Holly." Floyd pulled out an odd-shaped gun. It looked too thin and narrow to be real but the metal barrel gave up any illusion that it was a toy. "It's in his blood."

Holly stepped in front of Wade. "He's not Johnathan Lewis."

"The Lewis family were violent people a hundred years ago and they still are."

"You don't know him."

"You're infatuated with him, and that is messing with your head. But think about it. Can you honestly tell me you've never seen this man act violently?"

From his vantage point, Max could see Wade's fingers flex and tighten. Max glanced at the dented washing machine, and he caught Holly doing the same. Perhaps sensing a shift in his beloved, Wade pushed Holly aside.

"You are holding a gun on us," Wade said, chest puffed and teeth clenched. "You are threatening us at the same time that you accuse me of being the one who is violent."

"I'm not murdering anybody." Floyd leaned on the handrail to steady his aim. "But I will protect my sister."

While Wade remained calm, Holly lost her cool. "I didn't ask to be protected. And there's nothing wrong with Wade. He's a good man. The fact that you and all those others who are still keeping this grudge alive claim the moral high ground is disgusting. Wade went off and defended our country. I didn't see you crawling through the jungle. Oh, that may have been because you were too busy pushing papers and claiming that nobody would be able to take care of me in your absence."

"Just because you think you know all the answers, doesn't mean you do."

"And I suppose you're the expert on everything."

"I've had my eyes opened. That's why you can't be with this man."

"What the hell is that supposed to mean?"

Wade put his arm around Holly's shoulder. "It means that there is no reasoning with him. He's made up his mind." Wade stepped forward, bringing Holly with him. "I've seen this type before. Guys in Nam who had plenty of mouth, so sure of themselves, happy to tell you that they knew more than anybody else. But when it came time to pull the trigger, they discovered it wasn't so easy. Isn't that right, Floyd? You came here to kill the killer, but you haven't pulled the trigger yet. You really think you can kill both of us? Because that's what you'll have to do. Holly loves me. You shoot me in cold blood, and she'll hate you forever. She's not going to defend you or lie for you. In fact, she'll probably run straight to the police."

One side of Floyd's mouth rose. "I'm not going to kill you."

Too late, Max recognized the type of gun Floyd held. It came to him only due to watching too many nature documentaries — a tranquilizer gun. Floyd pulled the trigger and a yellow feathered dart sailed into Wade's chest.

As Wade fell against one of the dryers, Holly cried out. Though her words were garbled by her screams, Wade had been right — she intended to call the police. Floyd must have jumped to the same conclusion because he reloaded and shot Holly, too.

She stumbled forward, groping for Wade but weakening with every breath. Like a toy running low on batteries, her movements wound down until she lay still on the concrete floor.

Floyd darted out the door and returned with a brown paper grocery bag. He hastened down the stairs, set the bag on the folding table across from the washers and dryers, and pulled out several black candles. As he dug out two large containers of salt, the light began to dim.

Holly was losing consciousness, drifting into darkness, and that meant Max would drift along with her.

When light returned, it flickered in an amber glow — candlelight. The loop had not begun again. Holly's memory progressed towards the real terror that tormented her.

Still in the broom closet, Max had trouble discerning anything more than the candlelight. All else around him blurred like an out of focus camera.

"Don't move too fast," Floyd said. "It'll take a little bit until your head clears."

In the fuzzy distance, Max saw Holly attempt to sit up.

"He won't be waking." Hunched over the floor, Floyd placed the last of his candles. "I may have overestimated how much I needed to tranquilize him."

"Or you overestimated on purpose," Holly said, her words slurring together.

As the conversation continued, Holly's head cleared slowly, which allowed Max the ability to see more clearly, too. Floyd had moved Holly against the wall and left Wade against the dryer. Between the two, he had drawn a casting circle of salt and placed four candles at the compass points.

Wincing and rubbing the back of her neck, Holly frowned. "What is all this?"

Floyd crouched next to his sister. She cringed but he ignored her discomfort. "I know this seems crazy. I know you're mad at me. But please, remember that I'm your brother and that I love you. Please, trust me for a little bit."

"You shot me."

"I'm sorry about that. This will all make sense soon." He stepped over to his bag of supplies and checked a folded piece of paper. From the bag, he pulled out scissors and then approached Wade. Cutting off a lock of Wade's hair, Floyd said, "I want you to be happy. I want you to have everything you desire."

"Then stop. That's what I want. I desire Wade, so stop this."

Floyd set the lock of hair in the center of the casting circle. "She told me you would say that, told me everything that would happen here, and she was right."

"Who? What are you talking about?" Holly rubbed the sides of her head.

"I met a woman. I was upset about Wade and you, so I went

to a bar — I'm not proud of that, but it's important to be truthful in a relationship. I'm never going to lie to you. Never have and never will. This lady — I can't begin to explain what it felt like."

"I'm not a virgin. I know what it feels like."

Floyd wrinkled his nose. "Not that. She took me to her apartment and showed me magic."

"Are you talking about LSD? Or did she give you some pills?"

"It wasn't a drug trip. I know you think of me as your uptight, straight-laced brother, but I know a thing or two about marijuana and other things. Anyway, I didn't take any drugs. That's kind of the point. She showed me magic — the real thing. She made lights out of nothing and lifted us both off the ground. And then, she summoned a ghost."

As Max leaned forward and listened closer, Holly pressed back against the wall as if she could slide through it. "You're scaring me."

Floyd halted his preparations and gazed upon his sister as if she were a frightened puppy. "You are perfectly safe. This is going to help us. See, this lady knows all kinds of magic. She and I got to talking, and I told her about our problem with Wade being part of that terrible family. She understood right away, said she had met others like us, people who had come in contact with the descendants of Jonathan Lewis." Shaking his paper in the air, he went on, "She told me how to fix it. This spell she wrote down will summon the spirit of Jonathan Lewis and bind him to his descendent. All the ills created by that horrible murder, all the bad luck, all the evil forces — you call it karma, right? — it all will follow Wade. You will be free from him and I can take care of you. And one day, when Wade dies, the evil surrounding his family will finally be over. You understand now? I'm saving you, and I'm also saving all of the other descendants of Jonathan Lewis. I suppose it's a shame that Wade will have to be sacrificed, but we can end all the other suffering out there. You'll be safe. And I'll always be here for you."

Breathing hard, Floyd stood before Holly with an expectant look. Her eyes glistened as her head slowly turned from side to side. "You've lost your mind."

"It's okay," he said, kneeling before the casting circle. "I understand. It's a lot to take in. You'll see. When I'm done, everything's going to be okay."

Reading off his paper, Floyd whispered archaic words from dead languages. He held one hand over the center of the circle and repeated the words. Holly hugged her knees to her chest and tried to bury her head, but Max knew she peeked — otherwise, he would not see anything in her memory.

The candle flames burned brighter. The air surrounding Floyd's hand shimmered. With a sharp sizzle, the lock of Wade's hair ignited.

Whether from anger or fear, Max did not know, but Holly kicked out at her brother. Too far away to make contact, her foot swept across the floor. Right through the salt circle.

As the salt sprayed out in a wide arc, the candle flames rose high enough to lick the ceiling. Floyd cried out and stumbled back onto his elbows. One by one, the candles snuffed out. When the last one went dark, Max heard a dull pop like a metal pipe slamming down on a thick pillow.

Wade's head wracked to the side spraying blood across the dryer. Another dull pop and Holly's head jerked back painting the wall above her in a horrid fountain spray.

"No!" Floyd rushed over to Holly and cradled her against his chest.

Max kept expecting to feel the lurch forward and the rollercoaster drop, but it did not come. The truth dawned on him at the same moment that Floyd's desperate cries choked on his shock. Holly was still alive.

"Sis? Why did you do that? That was stupid. You ruined it." He stroked her bloodied hair as tears dripped off his nose and onto her forehead. "If you had just trusted me. You only had to sit there. Now look at this mess. The way I had it planned, everybody would have lived. But this — this is your fault. I wish you had listened to me. I love you, but you can be so stubborn. What am I supposed to do now?"

Sniffling his tears, Floyd gazed at the grotesque scene. Max could feel the change in the air. He had seen enough to understand the outcome and watched as Floyd made a terrible decision.

"I'm so sorry, Sis. I didn't want it to be this way." Scooting out from under Holly, he rested her on the floor. "It's too late for you and Wade, but I'm still alive. And I can't go to jail. Not for this, not for trying to do the right thing. For you. For Wade. For all of us. Forgive me."

Bending over, he locked his hands around her throat. With her brain cut open from magic and her senses reeling from tranquilizer, Holly had no way to defend herself. She never raised a hand, never moved a limb, never struggled at all.

It did not take long. As her life faded, so did the images before Max. The lurch came. The rollercoaster drop pulled him into darkness.

When he could see again, he stood on the opposite end of the laundry room, and Holly paced in anticipation of Wade's arrival. Max only had a few minutes. Once Wade entered, the memory would play out as it had for almost fifty years. No time for subtlety. He hoped Irene ended up okay after all of this.

"Holly, do you know me?"

She startled but quickly recovered — curiosity blending with a touch of recognition. Her eyes traveled the room as her left hand explored the top of her head, perhaps expecting to find the hole where her skull had burst open. "I'm having déjà vu, and it won't stop."

"That's because this is a memory. I don't have time to explain. I need you to reach out beyond this moment, try to feel where you really are."

Looking at her hands as she rolled her fingers, she said, "A memory? Where am I really?"

"You've attached yourself to my wife. You're part of her right now, and you are on the bed in my mother's apartment. Can you feel it?"

"Man, I don't know what you took, but I like the trip you're on."

Too late. Max could hear Wade opening the door. Grabbing Holly's hand, he said, "I'll be back here when all of this repeats. You must remember me. My name is Max. Remember that. Max."

He hurried to the broom closet. By the time he settled in and peeked out the door, Holly had resumed her role in her memory. It hurt to watch Floyd's botched spell destroy two innocent lives, but Max knew better than to interfere. Warnings aside, his own instincts told him that disrupting the natural flow of the memory too much could have disastrous results. If she began to believe that he was part of the memory, then she would never let him out.

The lurch. The rollercoaster drop.

"Holly, it's me, Max." Marching up to her, he put on a welcoming smile. "Do you remember?"

She squinted and picked at her nails, but she managed to nod.

"Good. Then listen to me — I've seen what happens. I know the truth now. I need you to set me free. I can save you, but I can't do it from inside your memory." He hoped his face looked honest. Most of what he said was true and he tried to focus on that. However, the part about saving her felt like a lie. He would try, he had the greatest lead he could ask for, but that guaranteed nothing.

"I don't want to die again. It hurts. Every time."

"If you keep me here, it'll never stop. But set me free, and there's a chance."

"And then what?"

"You move on. To whatever comes after."

"And he just gets away with it?"

"Wade is about to open that door. You've got to set me free now. If you don't, you'll die again and again and again. Forever."

She turned away and lowered her head. The lurch. The rollercoaster drop.

Max opened his eyes to find himself surrounded by his

mother, the Sandwich Boys, Irene Beck, and Drummond. On the bed, Sandra remained unconscious. His mother placed a tentative hand on his arm.

"I'm sorry," she said. "Maybe we can get this link to work some other way."

"It worked fine."

"But you just touched Irene's hand. Your eyes were closed for less than a second."

Max saw one confused face after another staring back at him. "I don't have time to explain. Boys, you stay here and help take care of everybody. Irene, thank you. You did it."

With the motion of his head, he indicated that Drummond should follow him. Drummond doffed his hat and floated through the wall. "You planning on explaining what happened?"

As Max left the apartment building and walked toward his car in the pouring rain, he said, "Floyd Claypool killed his sister. He screwed up a spell and caused this whole situation."

"Does that mean we're going where I'm thinking?"

"If you're thinking that I plan to confront Floyd Claypool, you're damn right."

Chapter 29

MAX CALLED FLOYD and demanded to meet with the man. At first, Floyd blustered his way through an argument, but when Max mentioned Holly and witchcraft, Floyd stopped talking. After a lengthy silence, he finally said, "I'll be at the park."

As Max drove, the rainstorm worsened. The other cars on the road became blurs of light floating on a black river. He wanted to floor the gas, race along the backroads, and screech his brakes as he pulled into the lot at the park. Instead, he gripped the wheel tighter as traffic slowed against the heavy downpour.

Taking twenty minutes longer than the drive should have, Max finally reached the park. He expected to find a chain blocking the gravel road leading toward the parking lot, but apparently Floyd had already arrived and left the chain off. The metronome beat of his windshield wipers played out as his wheels crushed the pebbled drive.

Drummond had remained quiet. But when they saw Floyd sitting in a green Corolla, he said, "That's odd."

"You thought he'd be standing outside, maybe under an umbrella, just waiting and getting soaked?"

"I thought he would have walked over to the pagoda. It's open but private."

"He doesn't want to talk with me in the first place. Maybe he's trying to make this as uncomfortable as possible in hopes of turning me away."

Drummond winced as if he ate bad seafood. "Stay here. I'll check out what he's got waiting for you." Only a few seconds later, he returned ready for a fight. "That bastard has a ghost ward. That's why he's staying in the car. Not because of the rain but because his ward protects him at about a ten foot radius."

"Then I guess I'm on my own." Max grabbed his umbrella.

"Be careful. I don't think he got a ward because of me."

"Holly?"

With a grave nod, Drummond said, "When a man has done wrong and lived with it for most of his life, he knows that eventually it'll catch up to him. I've seen it happen many times. You never know how they're going to react. Be ready for anything. Be careful."

The rain drummed against Max's umbrella as he crossed between the cars. Large puddles formed a minefield impossible to avoid. With both shoes soaked and water streaming off the ends of the umbrella, Max rapped his knuckle against the passenger side window. He heard the dull thunk of the door unlocking.

"Thank you for meeting with me," Max said as he squished into the passenger seat.

Floyd had the engine idling, the heat blowing, and the overhead map light on. His crooked nose cast an odd shadow down his face. "Only reason I'm here is to set you straight. Just because you've lived down here for a bunch of years doesn't make you a Southerner, so you might be forgiven for not knowing any better. The South — people down here don't forget easy. If you go spouting off about my sister and witchcraft, you'll be hurting my family name for generations."

"I'm beginning to see that."

"Then we have an understanding. Whatever you think you've learned, you need to keep it to yourself."

"We have a small problem about that." Rainwater trickled down Max's back, prickling his skin. "When you failed at casting your spell, you did more than kill Wade Johnson and nearly kill your sister. Some of that spell hung in the air. It was still there when you strangled her."

Floyd bristled. "I did not —"

"You created a torn ghost. You've locked Holly in a horror that will never end unless you help me. All I need from you is the name of the spell."

Setting his head back, Floyd sighed. It was not a sound of defeat or a sound of regret. Rather, Max heard a man making a decision that he knew had been inevitable from the start.

Floyd fumbled out a .38, snagging the hammer on his coat pocket, and pointed it at Max. He held the weapon close to his stomach as if trying to hide it from prying eyes. Perhaps he only wanted to hide it from his own.

"There's no need for that," Max said.

"There is, if you intend to cause me and my family problems."

"I'm only trying to help your sister."

"She's dead."

"She's suffering. I know you love her. Isn't that why you got yourself in this trouble? You wanted to protect her. Wade Johnson was going to take her away from you."

"Wade Johnson was a violent man from a violent family. Holly was naïve. She bought into the whole flower power thing. She really believed she could change the world, and I think she wanted to start with Wade. But you'd have an easier time solving problems in the Middle East than getting people to forget about the horrible things Jonathan Lewis did."

Max did not see a ward around Floyd's neck — probably carried it in his pocket. The chances of getting the ward and tossing it out the window were slim. Especially considering Floyd held a gun.

"He took everything from me." Though Floyd looked at Max, he clearly spoke to himself. "All those years I spent raising Holly, making sure she had food and clothing and shelter, taking care of everything, and that jerk waltzes in. I couldn't let him. I deserved better. Holly deserved better. I'd seen enough vets coming back from the war — no way could she fix him. Those boys were messed up in the head, their brains scrambled, and no amount of good intentions would solve their problems. What was I supposed to do? Sit back, let them get married, and wait until he snapped?"

Max's eyes locked on the weapon's muzzle. The more agitated Floyd became, the more the weapon moved about.

Not wanting to get shot accidentally, or on purpose for that matter, Max hoped to calm Floyd down and leave the car as fast as possible.

"I understand," he said, offering Floyd a sympathetic smile. "You never went to that laundry room to hurt your sister."

"I loved her. Still do."

"You didn't even want to kill Wade, did you?"

"Of course not. I'm no murderer. That spell was only going to curse him. I know that's not a great thing to say, but it also meant ending this feud against the Lewis family. Holly would've been mad at me, but she would've gotten over it."

"That's right. She loves you. And it's time to let the past go. Move on." Max had no idea if his words had penetrated Floyd's vacant gaze.

"You said she's still hurting?"

"Afraid so. She's stuck in a loop, getting strangled over and over."

"And it's my fault?"

"That doesn't matter anymore. You can't change what you did. But you can help her now. She should be free, and so should you."

Floyd lowered the handgun. "You should leave."

"I will, but first I have to know —"

"Leave now." He raised the handgun, higher this time, almost to Max's face.

"I can't," Max said, his words shaking, his heart racing. "My wife is in danger because of what you've done."

Floyd pulled back the hammer with his thumb. "I don't care if the whole world is going to burn. Get out of this car or I'll blow your head off."

Max paused. His mind raced for some angle with which to change Floyd's course of action, but he came up empty. He pulled the door handle and stepped out, not bothering to open his umbrella. As he slogged back towards his car, the rain drenching every inch of him, he could not stop thinking — *I've failed Sandra.*

He turned back. It couldn't end this way. He had to try

again, and if that meant taking a bullet, then at least he would die knowing he had done everything possible. But when he stepped toward Floyd's car, the windows flashed bright and the muted crack of a gunshot followed.

Max stared at the car. Part of him wanted to scream, rush over, and smash every window, slash every tire, destroy every trace of what Floyd had just done. But another part of him refused to move.

"Come on," Drummond said, hanging nearby. "Get in."

Max froze, bewildered by what he had seen. "It's over. He was our chance. Why'd he have to do that?"

"Stop acting like a baby. Nothing is over. Not if you get back in the car and get moving."

Pleased that Drummond would not be able to discern tears from rain, Max said, "What other lead do we have?"

"The ward. Each one is unique. Like handmade pottery. No two are exactly alike, and the artist always leaves a mark."

"You're saying witches sign their wards?"

"They don't intend to, but when you've walked into enough ghost wards, you start to recognize the different types of pain they cause. Especially when it's as strong as the one Floyd used."

Swallowing down any attempt at hope, Max said, "Do we have a lead or not?"

"Clear as a bell — so, get in your car and start driving. The last thing Sandra needs is for you to be caught out here when the police find Floyd's body. Suicide doesn't look much like suicide when there are people standing around acting guilty."

"Spit it out already! Who made that ward?"

Drummond swept in front of Max. "I'm not trying to toy with you. I just don't want you going off half-cocked like you did before when you thought you were going after Mother Hope."

"She did this? Mother Hope?"

"No."

Max's eyes widened. "The other ones?"

"Bingo. We're going to talk with the Mobley Coven."

Chapter 30

THE LAST TIME MAX sat in the living room of the Mobley Coven — the Coven of the Carolinas — he thought it *would be* the last time. At least, he had hoped so. This time, however, he knew he would find himself here more often than he ever wanted.

The house unsettled him. So well-cared for, so pristine and uncluttered, so unlike most of the witches he had ever encountered. Gentle curtains, expensive carpeting, light and playful paintings, and the smell of cinnamon in the air — all designed to give the image of an All-American family; all designed to obscure the truth about the home's residents.

Drummond entered through the ceiling after having toured the house. "Most of the witches are asleep. Lena is in the kitchen making tea — what is it with that woman and serving tea?"

"What about Grandma Mobley?"

Drummond did not have to answer. Lena Mobley entered carrying a serving tray with tea, and Grandma Mobley came in right behind. Jessica, one of the youngest in the coven, pushed Grandma Mobley's wheelchair until they reached a large fireplace on the far wall. With a short curtsy, Jessica left.

Lena set the serving tray on the coffee table and sat in an upholstered, high-backed chair. Crossing her legs before adjusting her dress, the middle-aged head of the coven gave Max a nod toward the tea. "Please, help yourself."

"I've had enough caffeine to keep me awake for a month."

Folding her hands gently in her lap, she said, "In that case, perhaps you can explain why you have arrived on my door soaking wet?"

"It's pouring outside."

"I think you know that's not what I meant."

"And I think you already know the answer." When it came to dealing with witches, Max had learned to walk a high wire between arrogant aggression and subservience — it worked best for him, keeping them off-balance.

Lena shifted a quick glance at Grandma Mobley. "We are truly saddened to hear what has happened to your wife. Sandra was a woman with great potential, and we had looked forward to watching her grow into her abilities."

"She's not dead. Before you act shocked, let's dispense with the little dance you love to do so much. I don't have time to play that game."

Drummond said, "Keep at them. They don't like your attitude but they haven't threatened you. That's a good sign."

Max agreed. However, Lena's restraint did not guarantee her help.

"It's late, Mr. Porter. Perhaps you should be direct, since that's the way you wish to be anyway."

"This is about Floyd Claypool. One of the Mobley Coven recently made him a ghost ward. As I drove over here, I got to thinking about that. A guy like Floyd — how would he have known to come here? Unless, he had been here before. The spell he messed up, the one that cursed his sister to be a torn ghost, I'd be willing to bet it came from here." Max cocked his head towards Grandma Mobley. "Isn't that right? Back in the 1970s, I think you provided Floyd with the spell."

Grandma Mobley's emaciated form shifted in her wheelchair. Lena nodded as if this communicated all she needed to know. "We would love to help you," she said before sitting back and grinning.

"Damnit!" Drummond threw his hat at the floor. "Nothing's ever free with witches."

"What do you want?" Max asked.

Lena traced her lips with her fingernail. "Mr. Claypool wanted a spell that would attach a ghost to a living being. Sort of like forcing a ghost to hunt a specific individual. He had some delusion that doing this would magically relieve the hatred in the hearts of so many. But it is not our duty to rid people of their delusions. He asked for a spell, and we provided. We warned him. It's a difficult spell and not one to be taken on by a novice. I'm not surprised to hear that he created a torn ghost. Sad though that it was the sister and not the Johnson boy. Not to mention the boy's friend."

"Friend?" Max closed his eyes as the last piece clicked into place. "You're the ones who cursed Donnie Blackwell's grave, and you were the ones intimidating ghosts in the Other."

"We wanted our involvement in this matter kept quiet, but Donnie's ghost visited us with threats of exposure." Lena edged forward with a light-hearted wink and a deadly tone. "Never a good idea to threaten a Mobley witch."

"What do you want?" Max asked again, speaking each word with slow impatience.

"Nothing."

"I don't believe that."

"Well, nothing at the moment. We will agree to break this unintended curse in exchange for the Porter Agency's assistance at a later date."

Simultaneously, Max and Drummond said, "No."

Max continued, "I can't agree to something so open-ended. Not with a witch. No offense."

Grandma Mobley chortled — a nauseating sound that quaked Max's stomach. Lena sat forward with her hands gripping the arms of her chair. "There is a battle coming. Mother Hope and the Magi think they can take the place of the Hull family. Their ambition is great, but they don't understand how badly the witches of North Carolina, of the world, no longer will tolerate being under the thumb of anybody. A day is coming, not too far away, and we do not intend to be on the losing side. When the time comes, we would benefit greatly if we had a spy in their midst."

Drummond floated down onto the couch. "Don't even think about it. You agree to this, and you'll end up no better than Leon Moore."

Max closed his eyes, tried to blot out the world. Drummond

was right, but Max saw little in the way of options. Still, being beholden to the Mobley's for the rest of his life was not going to happen.

"One time," he said. "If you free Holly Claypool, save my wife, then I will spy for you — but only one time. That's the best I can offer you."

Lena pursed her lips and attempted a frown, but her sense of triumph won over. "Only one time? Then it would have to be a time of our choosing. No matter when, no matter where. When we call on you, you will do the job we ask."

When dealing with witches, wording meant everything. "As long as the job is limited to spying, then yes."

Lena rose in a graceful motion and stepped behind Grandma Mobley. "We will discuss your offer." She wheeled the old lady out of the living room.

The moment the Mobley's left earshot, Drummond spun onto Max. "Have you gone insane? You can't do this."

"I don't know what else to do. We've run out of time."

"That's not true. It can't be. Sandra's strong. I'm sure she can hold out longer. Give us enough time to find a solution."

Max stood. If he had to sit any longer, he thought he might start throwing punches. "You weren't in Holly's memories. You didn't feel it. I'm telling you, that situation is falling apart. Heck, if it was just the torn ghost alone, I'd be worried. Being strangled by her brother over and over — there can't be any sanity left in that woman. But she's attached to Sandra, and that makes it a thousand times worse."

"I know, I know. Look, you've been around this crazy block enough times. Do you really think making a deal with witches as strong as the Mobley Coven makes any sense?"

"If it gets my wife back, then yes. And it'll only be for the one time."

Drummond drifted backwards towards the corner of the room. "You better hope to all that's holy they never call in that marker."

Grandma Mobley, Lena, and Jessica returned to the living room. Lena held a brittle, yellowed piece of paper with dark flowing script and Floyd Claypool's signature.

"We agree to the deal."

Max stepped closer. "Only one time of spying."

"That is correct. And we can demand that time whenever we choose."

"Okay then. Let's get this done."

Lena held the paper out at arm's length and ripped downward, cleanly tearing it in two. She placed both strips into the fireplace and watched them burn. As they curled into black snakes of ash, she returned to Grandma Mobley's side.

"That's it?" Max asked.

Jessica snickered from behind her hand. Lena shook her head. "That was only the contract between us and Floyd Claypool. We had to destroy that in order to unbind the curse." Lena spread out her arms and joined hands with the Mobleys at either side. "Now we will break the curse. You may want to stand back a little."

Drummond said, "Best to listen to the witch this time. It's not often they give you a friendly warning like that."

Max circled behind the couch and pressed his back against the wall. "Whenever you're ready."

All three Mobleys closed their eyes. Jessica stepped around so that she could join hands with Grandma Mobley. The moment their hands touched, the air within the physical circle they had created began to shimmer. While Grandma Mobley arched her head back and moaned in a sing-song pattern, Lena chanted words Max had never heard before — at least, he thought they were words.

Hovering next to Max, Drummond watched with a skeptical eye. "Sure didn't take them long."

"Huh?"

"They didn't need to consult a book or ask Grandma Mobley for details. Seems like they knew exactly what to do. Most witches I've ever met would need a few minutes to prepare first."

Max had hated the idea of making a deal with this coven, but Drummond's comment made him think the whole thing had been a set up. This turf war the Mobleys had started with Mother Hope had been in the making for a while. Max had no illusions about that. While he didn't think they had created the Holly Claypool situation for this purpose, they would be happy to take advantage of Max's misfortune.

"Yeah. I think you're right."

Drummond licked his lips and waved his forefinger at the side of his head. "Any more dealings with these ladies and you better be real careful. They've been playing chess for a long time while you thought we were all playing checkers."

"Makes me think that —"

A bright emerald ball of energy formed between the women before bursting outward. Max's muscles involuntarily constricted as the energy flew through him. Another emerald ball formed and as it shot off, Lena gasped. Sweat soaked the hairlines of all three women. A third ball emerged in the air and as it soared outward, Max's knees weakened.

Holding onto the window sill, he struggled to stay standing. It felt as if the air in the room had been burned away by hungry emeralds of magic. Another ball expanded outward. Max's head rocked back as if jabbed by an experienced boxer.

Jessica dropped to her knees but maintained a tight grip on her coven sisters' hands. The bright energy shot out at an ever-increasing rate. Drummond's coat fluttered back as if caught in a strong wind.

Catching Max's eye, Drummond said, "Don't worry about me. I can feel it, but I'm already dead. This magic can't do anything to me."

The next wave of energy slammed Drummond through the wall and out of the house. Though Max's ears rang, he still managed to hear Drummond's grumbling in the distance.

As Max climbed back to his feet, a crack formed in the window. He turned to face the witches. Several of the paintings on the walls had fallen to the floor. One of Lena's lovely sitting chairs had become a pile of scrap wood in the hallway.

Grandma Mobley sat in her wheelchair with her arms out stiff as if she had been carved from marble. Lena and Jessica, however, did not fare so well. They strained towards each other, desperate to keep their hands locked together. Even as Lena continued to chant her ancient words, a disheartening glaze covered her expression. Max could see it — she could not hold on.

Another emerald ball grew between the women. But this one behaved differently. It spun and wobbled. Lena's brow tightened as she tried to control the energy. Instead of pouring out in a powerful blast, the ball sputtered away toward the ceiling.

Jessica cried out and stumbled back a step. Her hands slipped, but Lena lunged toward her. Three fingers. That's all that kept Lena and Jessica connected.

That's all that's keeping Sandra from being lost forever.

Planting his hands on the back of the couch, Max vaulted over and landed next to Jessica. He grabbed her wrist, as well as Lena's, and pulled both women. Their palms pressed together. They laced their fingers tight.

Like holding a live wire, Max could not release his grip. The hairs on his arms stood straight up. His spine stiffened and he could smell chocolate. As he wondered *why chocolate?* the next emerald ball formed.

Everything went green. Wherever he looked, a green film covered the world. Even the air felt thick with green.

He saw himself standing on the opposite side of the circle holding Lena and Jessica by the wrists. But he saw it from a low angle — from Grandma Mobley's point of view. The two images superimposed as a third and fourth joined in — Lena and Jessica's viewpoints. All four of them could see and feel through each other.

As if moving through water, Jessica turned her head towards Max. Her hair floated around her and she smiled. For an instant, her face bore all the charm and innocence of Holly Claypool.

Max felt his head turn, drawn toward the center of their circle. The latest emerald ball of energy seemed larger than any of the others, and as it soared off in all directions, Max flew back into the couch. His mind told him he had been struck hard and fast, but his eyes witnessed everything at a languid pace.

"You okay?" Drummond asked, hovering above.

As Max stumbled to his feet, Jessica pushed Grandma Mobley out of the room. Lena patted her brow with a red hand towel. She folded the towel and placed it on the edge of the coffee table.

"It's done," she said. "Please leave."

"Not until I'm sure it really is over." Max dug out his cell phone and called PB.

Before PB spoke, sounds of celebration could be heard in the background. "I don't know how you did it, but you did it."

"She's okay?"

"She's awake and hungry. I think she's going to be fine."

"Let me talk with her."

"Hold on."

The few seconds it took PB to hand the phone over to Sandra lasted an eternity. But when she finally answered, Max's heart jumped. "Hi hon," she said.

It took all of his willpower not to break down crying. "I love you. Get some rest. I'll be with you soon."

She was exhausted, but they said a few more words before hanging up.

"Thank you," he said to Lena. "You all did a great job."

"We only did it because of the deal we struck."

"You ought to take the compliment. How often does a witch receive praise for her work?"

Lena chuckled. "I suppose."

"I'm just glad it's all over."

Lena's chuckle strengthened.

"What?" Max said, the easing knot in his stomach suddenly jerking tight.

"I was just wondering what an angry ghost like Holly might do now that she's free. All those years stuck in a loop — I expect it might drive one mad. Perhaps vengeance would be the recourse on her mind."

"She'll have a hard time with that. Floyd Claypool is dead."

She walked across the room and opened the front door. "Perhaps she'll take it out on his sons."

Max felt that rollercoaster drop, but this time he was in no memory. "He never mentioned any family."

"I should think not. He had the boys use their mother's maiden name — a pathetic attempt to hide them from us. But those boys were not going to sit back and watch their father fall prey to his youthful mistakes."

Drummond appeared in the doorway. "What's this witch blathering on about now?"

"I see it on your face," Lena said. "You're putting the pieces together. You're wondering about the ghost ward Floyd had. You were right that he would never come back here to get it. No, the man who hid his children, the man who killed his own sister and cursed her to an eternal torment, that man would never step foot in this coven's house again. So where did the ward come from?"

Max looked to Drummond. "The attacks on me. They were amateur, and they were attempting to keep us away from finding out about any of this. Floyd's sons did this. And that means one of them got the ward the day we found —"

"Yes?" Lena said. "Who made that ward? Which one of my sisters has betrayed us?"

"Sorry. That information isn't part of the deal we made."

"We could make another deal."

Drummond said, "If you do that, I will haunt you. And when you die and move on, I'll move on just so I can haunt you more."

"I think one deal with the Mobleys is plenty."

Lena pouted playfully. "What a shame. And here I was going to tell you what name those boys are using. By the time you go do your research and figure it out, Holly will be haunting them until she drives them crazy."

Max grinned. "Thank you. You just told me exactly who those boys are."

Chapter 31

HUMPED OVER AGAINST THE RAIN, Max scurried from his car to the open garage of the firehouse. A waterfall poured over the edge of a clogged gutter. Max shook off the rain, spraying it around like a wet dog.

"You sure about this?" Drummond said, poking his head around the garage. "Doesn't look like anybody's here."

"Both fire engines are here, so nobody's off fighting a fire. Somebody has to be here. What's wrong? Don't you trust me?"

"Usually. But you drove here like you were trying out for NASCAR, and I might add, you were on the phone with your wife the entire time. Not that a catastrophic auto accident is going to hurt me any, but I'd hate to see you die right after getting your wife back."

Softer, Max said, "I didn't want to stop hearing her voice."

"I'll give you this much — you were right not to tell her where you were going. She needs to rest."

"She needs to be safe, too. She's given enough to this case."

"Plus, you probably didn't want her running into her old love Peter again."

Max looked away. "Can we focus?"

With his hands on his hips, Drummond scanned the front of the garage. "You really think Owen and Chuck Williams are Floyd's sons? Sure, they're big lugs, and I even can see how they'd come at you hard with guns a-blazin' but then get scared and ease back each time after that — beyond that though, what do you really have?"

Ticking off the points on his fingers, Max said, "A slight family resemblance, the ghost wards, but most of all we have Holly's haunting. Why would she be haunting this firehouse if it didn't connect with her murder? This building is nowhere near the murder site. I think her ghostly energy was drawn here by the brothers. And they knew it, too. That's why they adamantly denied the existence of ghosts, and that's why they tried to get rid of anybody looking into it."

"I'm guessing you think we saw one of them leaving Bernice Mobley's spell shop."

"Somebody had to get the ward for Floyd. He wouldn't go to the coven house and he would've warned his sons not to go there either. They probably don't know much about the witch community, so they ended up at the first place they could find — and a Mobley is going to be one of the first to pop up on their radar."

"Right, because they're the strongest coven and the most powerful witches."

"After Mother Hope and the Magi. While that happened, the other brother set fire to my house."

"Okay, I'm convinced. So why are we still standing here?"

Max watched the door leading inside. "Because I don't hear anything. She has to be in there. She had a long head start."

"Either she's toying with her prey, or she's killed everybody in there."

"I suppose I could be wrong. If Owen and Chuck aren't Floyd's sons, then she'd have no reason to come back here. Everybody could simply be asleep."

"No sense in standing here shaking your knees. I'll check it out and report back."

Thrusting out one hand, Max said, "Stop. If you go in there and those boys have more active wards, you could be hurt. You're no good to me incapacitated."

"Thanks for your tepid concern, but I've faced worse than a ticked off ghost before."

"Just listen to me for once. If you walk in with me, you'll be able to feel the pressure of any wards building. You'll know when to stop. And without Sandra here, I can't see Holly. I can't gauge her reactions to the things I say."

Drummond smirked. "You need me."

Trying not to roll his eyes, Max said, "Fine. I need you. Can we go in together or do you still insist on blustering in and getting your head smacked hard by another ward?"

"Lead on." With one hand on his stomach and the other gesturing toward the door, Drummond made no effort to hide his mocking grin.

Max paused. He didn't want to give Drummond the satisfaction, but he had expected his ghost partner to go in first. As pride and doubt battled inside him, he reached for the knob and opened the door.

The long hallway stretched into shadows — the only light a dim amber in the kitchen at the far end. Max clicked on his flashlight and swallowed against his dry mouth. As he walked down the cold tiles, his footsteps tapped and the sound amplified in his mind.

Pleased that his flashlight beam remained steady, Max glanced over at Drummond. "You feeling anything?"

"Bored with the slow pace. Can't we move this along?"

"Sorry that I'm not rushing in brazen and foolish. I kind of want to survive tonight."

As they passed the captain's office, a voice whispered, "Psst. In here."

Max played his flashlight into the room. Captain Renner hid under his desk while Peter Rathburn lay beneath the cot in the back. As Max and Drummond entered the office, Renner motioned frantically for him to shut off the flashlight.

"You shouldn't be in here," Renner said. "Turn around and get out now while you can."

Max clicked his flashlight back on and checked both men's faces — frightened but not out of their minds with panic. Not yet. "What happened? What did you see?"

Renner shifted aside to allow Max a space to sit. "We're under attack. I didn't get an eye on the perp but he took Owen and Chuck hostage. He's also cut the phone lines and put up some kind of blocker. I can't get a call out. No demands were made, and when I tried to approach the kitchen, he hit me so hard, I flew back half the hallway. Never even saw it coming."

With a frustrated groan, Peter said, "That's because you

were hit by a ghost."

"I told you to put a lid on that crap. We got a serious situation here."

Drummond winked at Max. "Looks like you were right about the brothers."

"Is there anybody else in the building?" Max asked.

Renner said, "Mackenzie and Gates. They were in the rec room when it all started."

"Are they injured? Did you hear any screams?"

"Just Owen and Chuck. But they've gone silent." Renner gazed at Max, clearly hoping for any word that might suggest the brothers were still alive.

Max stood. "You two stay here. I'll handle this."

"You? This is a job for the police."

Before either man could make a false attempt at bravery in the shadow of the supernatural, Max said, "What's that they always say about you guys? Firefighters are the ones running into the fire while everybody else is running out. That's what I do with ghosts."

Thumbing back at Peter, Renner said, "You're just as bad as him. That's no ghost. It's some lunatic with a beef against my men."

"Captain, listen to him," Peter said. "He knows what he's talking about."

Max didn't have time for this. He stepped to the door, but Renner popped to his feet.

"Mister, I can't let you go out there."

"I'm real sorry about this," Max said. He nodded at Drummond, and the ghost swept in, plunged his hand into Renner's head, and rendered the captain unconscious. To Peter, Max added, "Stay here and look after him."

Max didn't wait for Peter's acknowledgment. He left the office and headed down the hall. When he reached the halfway point, he sent a questioning glance to Drummond.

"Not a single ward," the ghost said, massaging his hand.

"Stay close, and be ready for — heck, I don't know. Just be ready."

As they passed the rec room door, Max peeked in. Gates had backed into the corner but she wielded a fire ax. Mackenzie had a baseball bat in his hands as he took refuge behind the entertainment center.

"It's going to be okay," Max said. "Just stay tight and don't try to be heroes. Unless a fire breaks out. Then I'll need all the heroes I can get."

It felt weird to be acting the brave one in front of people who battled fire for a living, but in Max's world, feeling weird meant everything was normal. When he stepped into the kitchen, any sense of bravery fled from him.

Owen and Chuck floated in the air, one at each end of the table, their arms out as if crucified. Each wore a ghost ward around his neck, and each ward had been cracked in two. Owen's shirt had been shredded and blood trailed from his wounded chest down to his feet. Underneath Chuck, a yellow puddle had formed.

Owen had passed out, but Chuck lifted his head at Max's entrance. "You?"

"Is she in here?" Max asked Drummond.

"How should I know?" Chuck said. "She hasn't hurt either of us in at least ten minutes. Maybe she's gone."

Drummond nodded toward the center of the table. "She's right there." He took off his hat and pressed back his hair. "Hello, ma'am. I'm Marshall Drummond and this is my associate Max Porter. I imagine you don't want to recall your death ever again, but you may remember Max being there in your memory. He's the reason you're free from that nightmare." To Max, he said, "She says thank you and she is warning you to get the hell out of here."

"I can't do that." Max inched his way across the room.

Chuck said, "Can't do what? How about getting us down — you think you can do that?"

Max's eyes narrowed on Chuck. "You and your brother shot at me, roughed me up, and threatened the life of one of my kids. Do me a favor and shut up. You're making it awful difficult for me to want to save your life."

Lowering his head, Chuck whimpered. "I'm so sorry about that. I truly am. We were just trying to protect Papa. I didn't even believe in any of this magicky, voodoo nonsense. And we never meant to hurt you or your kid. We only wanted to scare you."

"Is that why you burned my house down?"

"Owen did that. I wasn't even there. I was out getting these stupid ghost wards that didn't even work. Owen — he always was the true believer. He'd do anything for Papa."

Drummond said, "She's laughing. I think she's enjoying seeing Chuck blubber like this." With a smooth glide, he moved closer toward Holly. "Listen. I know where you're coming from. I was cursed for over seventy years. Max here and his wife, Sandra — they're the ones who saved me, just like they saved you. I understand the urge for revenge. But believe me, it doesn't go away. The people who hurt me are all dead, and I still feel empty inside. But hey, we're ghosts. We kind of are empty inside."

Drummond's face dropped. Max froze. "What's wrong? What's she doing?"

"Um, pal, I don't think she's too appreciative of what you did."

"What did I —"

Max felt a sharp pain as if two icy meat hooks dug in under his ribs. He arched back and was hoisted four feet into the air. Against his will, his arms shot out to the sides.

"Hang in there," Drummond said. "Sorry, bad choice of words." He spun back to Holly. "Don't do this. I know you've been through something horrible, but you still have a chance to move on. You don't have to be stuck here as a ghost for eternity. If you keep doing this, that chance will disappear."

Drummond's head whipped to the side and his body shot across into the refrigerator. He soared back with his hand clenched into a fist and swung. Owen's body turned as Holly rammed through him.

"Lady, we are trying to help you. But I swear if you hit me again —"

Drummond doubled over before shooting straight up through the ceiling.

"We're going to die," Chuck said, tears streaming down his cheeks.

Max wanted to offer encouragement but the cold spreading over his torso made him reconsider. Chuck might be right.

Careening to the ground, Drummond's arm appeared to hook Holly and throw her hard against the floor. Max had seen his partner fight before but never with such vehemence. He understood. The ghosts they had fought in the past chose to do wrong. But Holly was the victim. Max suspected Drummond wanted to end the fight as fast as possible, not only to save Max but to get Holly to move on — even if that meant fighting harder than usual.

But Drummond jerked back, flipped over, and crashed into the ground. He repeatedly shook his head as if unable to focus. A long groan escaped his lips.

Max saw it in Drummond's eyes — a crazed, ex-torn ghost had nothing to lose. She would kill them all. But Max heard the sharp click of footsteps. Despite the pain of moving any of his muscles, he lifted his head and gazed down the hallway. He thought he might be hallucinating. But then Sandra entered the kitchen with Irene Beck at her side.

Sandra set her fists on her hips, raised her chin, and like a mother scolding a bratty child, she said, "Holly Millicent Claypool, sit your ass down right in front of me or you are in big trouble."

Chapter 32

DRUMMOND FLOATED UP NEXT TO MAX, his mouth dropped wide open. "She did it. Holly stopped fighting me and is sitting in front of Sandra."

Max wanted to cheer his wife on, but his arms remained locked apart. Despite the pain running along his sides and the muscles of his back, he watched Sandra with a smile on his face.

"For such a bright, young girl, you sure are doing stupid things." Like a game show hostess presenting the latest prizes, Sandra gestured to the men floating in the air. "Let's start with you letting them down. Easily."

Max, Owen, and Chuck drifted downward until their feet touched the floor. Their arms released, and Max felt the icy hooks in his chest disappear. Still unconscious, Owen collapsed to the floor. Chuck stood with his arms stiff at his sides and his eyes locked open — he would need serious PTSD counseling, but for the moment, Max had no fear of Chuck interfering.

Sandra snatched a peek at Max. She had a role to play and couldn't risk undermining it with any greater expression. He gave her a nod and mouthed *You've got this.*

"I know how angry you are," she said. "I know everything about you. When you linked with me, you opened your entire existence to me. Even if I didn't want to know, it's all up in my head now. Do you understand? Every moment of your life that you can remember is a memory in me now. So, when I tell you that I understand the hatred you have towards your brother and his offspring, I truly know.

"But, I'm guessing from your behavior, that this transfer of memory did not go both ways. If it had, you would know that your actions are going to destroy any chance you have towards a happy future."

Drummond flew over to face Holly. With a patronizing glare that Max knew too well, Drummond said, "I've been trying to tell her that. If she goes hurting Owen and Chuck, she'll only be dooming herself."

"He's right," Sandra said. "And believe me, we don't like to admit he's right about anything."

Max pulled back a chair and sat. The moment he felt his body relax, however, he was thrust into the air once again. His arms snapped out straight.

"You let him go now," Drummond said, pulling back a fist.

Sandra dropped to her knees. "Please, please, look at me. Look in my eyes. That's the man I love. You can see it in me because I know how you feel about Wade. That's how I feel."

Max's eyes teared. His chest hurt with a pain not caused by Holly's icy hooks. He wanted to call out, to tell Sandra he felt the same. Of course, she knew already, but he had to shout it. Yet when he opened his mouth, Holly locked onto his throat.

Drummond moved closer. "I've been doing this ghost gig a lot longer than you. I know ways to hurt you like you wouldn't believe."

With a gentle motion, Sandra asked Drummond to sit back. "Holly, look at me. That's right. I know what's in your heart, and it's not only anger. There's love inside you. You love Wade. That's what this has always been about. Floyd loved you and he couldn't bear the thought of you loving anyone else. Don't do the same thing. Don't kill the one I love because you have been hurt."

Max tried to focus on the events below him. He knew his fate hung in the results of that conversation, but his vision blurred and his mind clouded. He had to stay conscious. He had to stay awake no matter how inviting the idea of rest without pain.

"You might still be able to have what you want." Sandra's voice had taken on a desperate tinge. "I can't guarantee anything because anybody who's moved on has never come back."

"Actually," Drummond said.

"You didn't move on, not like this. And you're not helping. Holly, if you stop hurting my husband, stop hurting everybody, and let Irene guide you, there is a chance you will find happiness. When Wade died, he died clean. He did not become a torn ghost, he was not locked in a loop of suffering, none of that. By interrupting Floyd's spell, you saved the man you love even as you set up your own torture. But now, follow Irene and you will move on to the same place Wade did. If any of the lore is true, then he will be there waiting for you with open arms. And if your love for him is half as strong as what I have with Max, then you have all eternity to share with each other in bliss."

Like bursting through the ocean surface, Max's lungs gasped for air. He heard a cry and felt arms wrapped around him as his body lowered to the chair. Though his sight remain blurred, he knew the scent, he knew the warmth of skin, he would know her anywhere — his love, his Sandra.

As Irene talked Holly through the process of moving on, Sandra helped Max walk down the hallway. Drummond floated right behind.

"It'll be okay in a few minutes," she said as they passed the captain's office. "When Irene walks out, you'll have no more problems here. Owen and Chuck will need your help."

"Doll, you were incredible in there." Drummond clapped his hands once. "I wasn't so sure Holly would buy what you are selling, but you sure stuck to it."

"If she hadn't, I would've cast every spell I knew to rip her apart." She gave Max a tight squeeze. "Nothing gets between me and my husband."

Peter stepped into the hall. "It's really over?"

Max straightened. "It's over. We'll send you our bill."

"Thank you. Both of you. Sandra, let me take you out to dinner to show you my appreciation."

She laughed. "It's been real nice reliving our old times, but I've had enough of memories for a while."

As they got into the car, Max said, "Thanks for rescuing

me."

"I'm your wife. Besides, you think I want to run this business with the ghost? I need you."

"Thanks nonetheless."

Rolling her neck from side to side, she said, "I just want to go home and have a nice hot bath."

"Yeah. About our house ..."

Chapter 33

THREE DAYS LATER, Max, Sandra, Drummond, and Irene stood at Holly Claypool's grave. Her brother, Floyd, had the plot next to her, but Irene promised that Holly had moved on and would not be bothered by Floyd's presence.

"Such a sad waste of life," Irene said. "We really must do our best to make the most of the time we have."

Max thought of his mother and the Sandwich Boys. For them, life had returned to its predictable routine. The boys had their schooling, Mrs. Porter had her teaching, but Max could tell there had been a change. Everybody seemed closer now. His mother even offered Sandra a complement — she said Sandra made good coffee.

Baby steps.

With a salute, Irene dropped her voice low. "Goodbye, Holly." She turned to leave but paused. "If you ever need my help again, don't hesitate to call. Y'all are fun."

Drummond clicked his tongue. "You're not half-bad yourself."

Staring straight at him, Irene said, "Aw. Coming from you, I'll take that as high praise." Everybody stared at her. "I'm psychic, not stupid. After you scared me in my shop, I took the time to tune into your frequency — that's how I think of it, anyway. Besides, no way can a hunk like you can hide from me."

"Well, sweetheart," Drummond said, sliding alongside her, "seems to me that you and I have a lot to talk about. If I could drink, I'd offer to buy you one."

Irene tittered. "Mr. Drummond, are you flirting with me?"

The two continued playfully as they walked back toward Irene's car. Max put his arm around Sandra and spent a final moment staring at the grave. "I know we've come close to losing each other before, but I've got to say, this time had me really scared."

"Me, too."

"I think we're going to have to tell the boys the truth. Maybe my mother, too. I don't like the idea that if one of us dies, the other will have to continually lie about it to those that we love."

Sandra leaned in against him. "I had the same thought."

He tried to feel comfort holding her, but a hard stone formed in his throat. "There's a war coming. These witches — I don't see how there can be peace between them."

"I've read about these things. Witch wars smolder for centuries, and when they finally ignite, a lot of people end up dead. Or worse."

"That's what I'm afraid of. Especially because there's no way around it. We're caught in the middle. That's another reason why we need to clear the air with those we love."

"Absolutely. But first we need to clear the air with each other."

"About what?"

"For starters, you need to admit that you were jealous of Peter."

Even though Sandra kept her face low and away from Max's view, he knew she smiled. "I wouldn't use the word jealous, but I certainly didn't trust the guy. I suppose I could've been nicer."

"You were so jealous that I think Drummond started making sense to you."

Max chuckled. "Okay. But why wouldn't I be jealous? The woman I love getting all starry eyed over an old boyfriend."

"Oh, honey, sometimes you are very thick. Peter Rathburn was never a real boyfriend. We were teenagers, and we didn't want to be the only ones not dating. We wanted to have somebody to go to the prom with. We were friends, but that's it."

"Really? Not friends with benefits?"

She smacked his chest. "What kind of girl do you think I

was back then? Don't answer that. Besides, Peter's gay."

"What?"

"You really couldn't tell?"

"Not in the least."

"Yup. So I hope you're happy with me because you're stuck with me." She looked up at him. "We'll get through this. We always do."

"Something tells me this is going to be harder than getting rid of the Hulls. More dangerous, too."

"Doesn't matter. Together, we can take them on. Push straight on through. Just like always."

Max leaned over and kissed her firmly on the lips. He gazed into her eyes and said nothing more. Nothing more needed to be said.

Afterword

Thanks for joining me, Max, Sandra, Drummond, and the whole family for another fun mystery. I hope you enjoyed it as much as I did. I know that y'all love to get some behind-the-scenes scoop about the history, so here it is:

As you may have realized, the story of Naomi Wise is true. All of it. Including the Bob Dylan song which you can find a scratchy recording of on YouTube. The only liberty I took with the story was imagining that the descendants of Johnathan Lewis might still be connected with it all. And while, as far as I know, there is no long standing feud reaching to the present day, there have been places named of Naomi as I mentioned in the story. There have been books written about her murder over the centuries, so if you're really curious, check those out.

The side note about George L'Estrange being arrested for murder, treated well in prison, and finally pardoned is also true. North Carolina has a long history of justice done in this way.

For those of you who live in High Point or know the area, you'll note that I changed the geography slightly. Across from the YWCA and sandwich shop is a parking lot and medical offices. I wanted a dark alleyway and so I plunked it down there.

That's all for now.

Acknowledgements

This book took a while to happen. Originally, I had intended to have the climax of one of the earlier books to be at a firehouse. I had met one of the Chiefs on a flight to Charlotte and figured I could make something work with what he did for a living. Through this great guy (they all asked that I not single anybody out and rather give credit to them all), the awesome folks of the Winston-Salem Fire Department allowed me to come in, check out a firehouse, and interview several of the firefighters. I came away with so much to work with that I realized I would make an entire book around them. And that's what I did. So, a BIG thank you to all the men and women of the Winston-Salem Fire Department for their generosity and their willingness to do such dangerous work.

I also want to thank the incredible Claudia Ianniciello for yet another great cover, and to my son for unending support. Special thanks to my launch team for their tireless reading. And double-special thanks to my wife for helping me make my deadline (this book almost had to hold off for a month).

Always, I hold my dearest thanks to you, my reader. My life and Max's life grow with every book, and we couldn't do it without you. Thank you.

About the Author

Stuart Jaffe is the madman behind *The Max Porter Paranormal Mysteries,* the *Nathan K* thrillers, *The Parallel Society* series, *The Malja Chronicles, The Bluesman, Founders, Real Magic,* and so much more. His unique brand of old pulp adventure mixed with a contemporary sensibility brings out the best in a variety of SF/F sub-genres. He trained in martial arts for over a decade until a knee injury ended that practice. Now, he plays lead guitar in a local blues band, *The Bootleggers,* and enjoys life on a small farm in rural North Carolina. For those who continue to keep count, the animal list is as follows: one dog, two cats, three aquatic turtles, nine chickens, and a horse. As best as he's been able to manage, Stuart has made sure that the chickens and the horse do not live in the house.

www.ingramcontent.com/pod-product-compliance
Lightning Source LLC
Chambersburg PA
CBHW030530310726
48979CB00010B/1866/J
9781963517033